A Second Chance at Love

Karon Curtis

PAGE PUBLISHING
Conneaut Lake, PA

First originally published by Page Publishing 2022

ISBN 978-1-6624-4811-9 (pbk)
ISBN 978-1-6624-4812-6 (digital)

Printed in the United States of America

For Mom and Dad

1

Jade filled her journal with the things she wanted to do and have accomplished at different stages in her life. But she soon found out that life, in and of itself, had a way of throwing curveballs at you.

And life did just that. According to Jade's list of goals, meeting someone and falling in love was not supposed to happen now. That was like number seven on her list. But all the same, Jade met Connor and fell in love with him.

Jade was happy to be in love, but she felt bad for keeping her relationship with Connor from her parents. Jade had promised her parents that she would not get involved with anyone until after she graduated from college. So against her better judgment, Jade kept Connor a secret from the people she trusted and loved the most, her family.

Connor wasn't her only secret. After graduation, she and Connor had plans to get an apartment, and that was a bigger secret. In all the conversations she had with her parents, she failed to tell them about Connor and the apartment.

Jade's parents were expecting her to move back home after graduation, but she had other plans. And she had no idea how they were going to accept her news.

Thankfully, Jade's love for Connor was greater than her fear of telling her parents the truth. Jade loved Connor, and she would find a way to make her parents realize that.

One thing, however, did work in her favor. Her parents liked Connor, a lot. Not because he came from a wealthy family but because he was a good friend to Jade.

Connor hit it off with Jade's parents from the first time they met him. His warm presence and captivating smile stole their hearts just as it did Jade's. Mr. Simpson felt quite comfortable about Connor that he asked him to keep an eye on Jade at school. Little did Mr. Simpson know, Connor was already fulfilling the task.

For Connor, it was easy. He knew he liked Jade from the moment he saw her. He would never forget the night their eyes met. Connor wondered who she was, sitting alone and glowing in the darkness. He had to meet her.

Ever since Connor was a young boy, he knew he would work in the family business whether he liked it or not. Good for his parents, he liked it.

Connor found pleasure in telling Jade countless stories of how his family found old, run-down properties and turned them into beautiful pieces of real estate. At the end of the day, Connor knew that a family would have a home and that pleased him tremendously.

2

Jade and Connor had breakfast at the corner café before her hair and nail appointment. She wanted to look her best on her graduation.

"Thanks for breakfast, Connor. It was delicious."

"My pleasure," said Connor. "What time is your appointment?"

"Ten thirty," replied Jade. "After that, I'm going to finish packing up my dorm so my parents can take some of my junk home with them."

"Well, I'm just about done packing, so I'll stop by later and help you finish up."

"That would be great," said Jade.

Jade leaned over the table and gave Connor a kiss. Connor pulled a few dollars out of his wallet and placed the money on the table. Then he stood up, grabbed Jade's hand, and walked with her out of the café and to her car. Connor opened the driver's side door for Jade and helped her inside the car. Jade rolled down the window, and like he always does, Connor leaned in and gave Jade a kiss.

"See you later, baby. Gotta go," said Connor.

"Okay. I'll call you when I get back to my dorm."

"Okay. Be safe. *Ti amo*," said Connor.

"Love you too!"

By the time Jade arrived at the salon and sat in Alexa's chair, her mind was made up. She had decided to get her curls straightened out and add some highlights. Connor loved Jade's curls and she hoped that he would like her new hairdo. Sometimes Connor would press his face into Jade's curls and make her laugh.

"Okay, Ms. Jade, what are we doing today?" Alexa asked.

"I want something different," replied Jade.

"Oh really! How different?"

"Let's straighten out my curls and add some highlights," replied Jade.

"Now that is different, and I think that will look nice on you," Alexa said.

"Sweet," said Jade. "I'm ready."

After Jade's hair was done, she looked in the mirror and smiled. Jade jumped out of the chair and gave Alexa a big hug.

"Thank you, Alexa. I love it," shouted Jade.

"You're welcome, sweetie. And congrats on your graduation. Shia will be ready to do your nails in a minute."

"Great," said Jade. "I have time for a bathroom break. Be right back."

Jade took a few selfies of her new look and sent them to Sophia and Becca. She was going to send Connor a picture too, but she decided against it. She wanted Connor to see her new do in person.

"Hey, Shia, how you doing?" Jade asked.

"Good," replied Shia. "How are you?"

"Excited," replied Jade. "I can't wait for tomorrow."

"I bet," said Shia. "Well, c'mon and sit down. I'm ready for ya."

"So what do you want done today?" Shia asked.

"Something cool and fresh," replied Jade.

"Well, I can do that," said Shia. "What colors do you want for the nail art?"

"Surprise me!"

"I gotcha covered."

Shia put on her gloves and mask and got to work on Jade's nails. An hour and a half later, Jade's nails were done, and they looked awesome. After Jade paid for her hair and nails, she headed back to her dorm and called Connor.

"Hey, I'm heading back now."

"Okay. I'm finishing up here, and then I'll be over."

"Okay, see you later," said Jade.

"Do you want me to bring you anything?" Connor asked.

"Yes," replied Jade. "A medium pizza, with sausage, from Vinny's."

"Got it. See you in a bit, baby. Love you."

"Love you too," said Jade.

As soon as Jade arrived at her dorm, she wrapped her hair in a silk scarf. Jade was determined not to sweat her hair out while she finished packing her things. While Jade waited for Connor, she put a few boxes together and stored some of her belongings. She made sure to label the boxes and was extra careful to put the boxes going home with her parents on one side of the room and the boxes going to her new apartment on the other side of the room.

"Knock, knock," said Connor as he entered the room. "I have a delivery for Ms. Simpson."

"That would be me, sir," said Jade. "How much do I owe you?"

"Just a kiss right here," replied Connor as he pointed to his lips.

"Thanks for the pizza," said Jade.

"My pleasure! Now do me a favor and take off that scarf. I want to see your hair."

Jade pulled the scarf off her head and swung her head to the left and right.

"Wow," said Connor. "Your hair looks great. I love your curls, babe, but this straight look is so sexy."

"Stop it, Connor."

"I'm serious," said Connor. "You look stunning! Did you have enough money?"

"Yes. And thank you," said Jade.

Jade grabbed the pizza box and set it on her desk. She grabbed two paper plates off the bookshelf and two bottles of water from the fridge. Then she and Connor sat down and ate.

"You got a lot done in here," said Connor.

"Sure did," said Jade. "Just a little bit left to do, and I'll be done."

"I'll make you some more boxes after we eat."

"Cool," said Jade.

"I can't wait until this graduation is over," said Connor.

"Why? Tomorrow is going to be awesome," said Jade.

"I know, but Sunday is going to be even better because we move in to our own place. We can stay up as late as we want, play music as loud as we want, have as many parties as we want, walk around naked, and make love whenever and wherever we want to."

"I'm not trying to have a lot of parties," said Jade, laughing. "And staying up all night, not gonna happen. I need my beauty rest," she joked.

"You sure don't need that. You *are* beauty," said Connor as he planted a kiss on Jade's cheek.

"Stop flirting with me. I'm already yours," said Jade.

"Yes, you are," said Connor. "Are your parents okay with us living together?"

"I haven't told them yet," replied Jade.

"What! Why not?"

"Because they are not going to like it, Connor."

"Jade, just tell them. They might be upset at first, but they'll get over it."

"You don't know my parents that well. They don't condone pre-marital shacking."

"But they know we're together, so what's the big deal?"

Jade looked disturbed. How was she to tell Connor that her parents didn't know that she was in a relationship with him?

"What's with the look, Jade?"

"They don't know that either," she replied.

"Are you serious? I thought we agreed to tell our parents months ago."

"I know, but I couldn't," said Jade. "My parents didn't want me getting involved with anyone while I was in college, and I promised I wouldn't. Then I met you, and…"

"So your parents still think that I'm just a friend?" Connor asked.

"Pretty much," replied Jade.

"You said that very casual, Jade, like it doesn't matter to you."

"It does matter, Connor. It matters a lot. I will tell them. I just need a little bit more time."

"For God's sake, Jade. We're moving in together. I would say that time is up."

"I'm sorry, Connor. Please don't be upset."

"I'm not upset, Jade, just annoyed that you haven't told them yet."

Connor rolled his eyes and shook his head. He silently helped Jade pack the rest of her books and clothes. Before they knew it, they were finished.

Jade rubbed her hands together as she visually inspected her room.

"Finally done!" she exclaimed.

Jade glanced over at Connor and noticed that he was still annoyed. She grabbed her phone, tapped on the music app, and played Connor's favorite song. Jade walked over to Connor and stood in between his legs. She brushed his hair with her fingers and cradled his cheeks in her hands.

"I'll tell my parents tomorrow. I promise."

Connor stood up, smiled, and gave Jade a kiss.

"You know that's my song, right?"

Jade smiled and said, "That's why I played it. Do you feel better now?"

"Not quite, but I got a feeling I will soon."

Jade and Connor danced to the sounds of Usher's "Love in this Club." Jade loved the way Connor danced. Aside from his dashing smile, his smooth moves excited her. Jade's thoughts went back to the night they met.

* * *

It was a hot August night, and Jade was overwhelmed preparing for her final year at VCU. After she unpacked a few of her things, she wanted to go out for a drink. She had just turned twenty-one and was still in party mode.

After contemplating for thirty minutes, she jumped in the shower and did her hair and makeup. Jade wanted to look nice and classy. She decided to put on her white shorts and her sexy gold top that hung off her shoulders. To complete her outfit, she added a simple gold necklace, nothing too alarming, just soft enough to accent her neckline. She sprayed her glitter body spray on her chest to get the glitter effect that she liked. She found her cute white sandals in an unpacked box and stepped into them. Then she took one last look at herself in her full-length mirror, grabbed her white pouch, and ran out the door.

At Club Paradise, Jade treated herself to a drink, finally able to show a real identification card. She found an empty table, sat down, and watched her fellow colleagues mingle and grind on the dance floor.

She shook her head and sipped her drink. When she looked up, her eyes locked with a handsome guy standing across the room. She wished Sophia and Becca were at the club to help keep her calm.

As he walked toward her, she got nervous and began to question herself. Should I get up and leave? Should I act like I'm on my cell or what? *And still, Jade couldn't take her eyes off him. He was the one, and she felt it.*

"Excuse me," he said in a sexy voice. "Is this seat taken?"

"No," replied Jade.

"May I join you?"

"Sure."

"My name is Conario Ellis," he said.

"Conario?"

"Yes, it's Italian. My friends call me Connor. What's your name?"

"Jade. Jade Simpson."

Jade and Connor talked for hours that night. He made her laugh and smile. He even bought her a drink. He asked her to dance, and she accepted. His cologne was hypnotizing, his gentle touch on the small of her back was enticing, and she thanked God that his breath smelled good.

* * *

"You seem deep in thought. What's up?"

"Nothing," replied Jade. "So how do you feel now?"

"A lot better," whispered Connor.

"I bet you do." Jade laughed.

"You know you could have told me that you were scared to tell your parents about us."

"I wasn't scared. I just wasn't ready to tell them," said Jade.

"Scared, not ready, whatever," said Connor. "Those are excuses. If it'll make you feel better, we can tell them together."

"Connor, I appreciate that, but I want to tell them myself."

"Before or after graduation dinner?" Connor asked.

"Before," replied Jade.

"Okay. Now give me some of that tongue."

Jade laughed and gave Connor a long tongue kiss.

3

When Jade's name was called, she stood up and walked across the stage, smiling from ear to ear. She was elated to finally finish college and get her bachelor's degree. Now she had to figure out what she was going to do with it. Her immediate plan was to continue working at Five Star Marketing and gain more experience so that one day, she can own her own marketing firm.

Jade looked into the crowd and saw her family standing and clapping for her accomplishment. She saw her father, with his iPad in his hands, recording her every step. She saw Justin and his wife, Zaria, cheering for her and taking her picture. And then she saw her mother, wiping her tears away. Jade was overjoyed.

After the ceremony, Jade met her family in the lobby. They hugged and kissed her, gave her a bouquet of roses, and took lots of pictures.

"Congratulations, sweetie," shouted her mother. "You look beautiful! And the ceremony was very nice."

"Thanks, Mom. I'm glad it's finally over."

"We are so proud of you, young lady," said her father.

"Thanks, Dad. I'm glad I didn't waste your hard-earned money."

"Me too." Her father chuckled.

"Girl, what did you do to your hair?" Justin asked.

"Justin, leave her alone," said Zaria. "Her hair looks nice."

"Thanks, Zaria," said Jade.

"Don't pay your brother any mind," said Zaria. "He's just mad because he's baldheaded."

After Jade and her family took pictures, they met up with Connor and his family and exchanged introductions. After the introductions, Jade and her family took pictures with Connor and his family. Then Jade's father and Connor's father stepped away for a manly conversation.

"I can see where Jade gets her beauty from," said Julia.

"Thank you," said Tanya. "It's a pleasure to finally meet you and Gordon."

"Same here," replied Julia.

"I see my dad is talking your husband's ears off," said Jade.

"Hah. Don't worry, dear. My Gordon loves to talk," said Julia.

Jade and Connor laughed.

"Your son has been an incredibly good friend to Jade. She called us many nights, telling us how much Connor helped her with her studies. I really appreciate Connor for doing that."

"I'm sure he didn't mind," said Julia. "He loves helping people."

"I can tell," said Tanya. "We're looking forward to breaking bread with you and Gordon this evening."

"Oh yes, dear. We can't wait. We're going to have a great time," said Julia.

Jade and Connor smiled as they watched their parents get acquainted. Connor wanted to hug Jade, kiss her, hold her hand, but he couldn't do any of those things. Connor would have to wait until Sunday, when he and Jade would be all alone in their new apartment, and he would have Jade to himself.

"I want a picture with my bestie," yelled Sophia as she ran toward Jade.

"Hey, we did it," shouted Jade as she hugged her friends.

"Yes, we did," said Becca. "And congratulations to you too, Connor."

"Same to you, ladies," said Connor as they exchanged hugs and kisses.

"Let's move over there so I can take a few pictures of y'all," said Connor.

Jade handed Connor her phone, and she and her friends posed as Connor took their picture.

"Send me all those pics," said Sophia.

"I sure will," said Jade.

"We better go say hello to your mom," said Becca. "She looks frigging good by the way."

"You better." Jade laughed.

Sophia and Becca kissed Jade and walked over to Mrs. Simpson.

"Excuse us," said Becca. "Mrs. Simpson, we just wanted to come over and say hello."

"Hey, girls," said Mrs. Simpson. "How are y'all doing?"

"We're doing well," replied Becca.

"You must be Connor's mom?" Sophia asked. "He looks just like you."

"I am," replied Mrs. Ellis. "And congratulations on your graduation."

"Thank you," said Sophia.

"Now, when are you girls coming back to visit me?" Mrs. Simpson asked.

"Hopefully soon," replied Sophia.

"Okay. I'm going to hold you to that," said Mrs. Simpson.

Sophia and Becca hugged Mrs. Simpson and went to mingle with their fellow graduates.

Louis and Gordon finally made their way back to the lobby. Jade stared at her father, searching for a hint of what he and Gordon talked about. Her father looked happy, which meant that they didn't talk about her and Connor shacking up, and that was a good thing for Jade.

"Well, we better get going," said Tanya.

"Sounds good to me, Mom."

"Mr. and Mrs. Ellis, we'll meet you at the restaurant," said Tanya. "We made reservations for six o'clock."

"That'll be fine," said Julia. "See you all later."

The adults shook hands. Connor gave Jade a hug and kissed her on her cheek.

"See you later," he whispered.

* * *

Back at the dorm, Louis and Justin began taking Jade's boxes downstairs. Tanya sat on the bed, instructing Jade and Zaria on what to do in the room. When Jade and Zaria were done, they sat down and rested.

"So I see you decided to get rid of your curls," said her mother.

"Yep," said Jade. "I wanted something different for graduation. Do you like it?"

"It's nice, but I like your curls," replied her mother.

"You know I like to experiment Mom. Who knows, I might just cut all my hair off one day."

"You better not," yelled her mother.

"I think she's joking, Mom," said Zaria.

"She better be," said her mother. "How's work?"

"Surprisingly good," replied Jade. "My supervisor said that I may get a raise once I graduate. So I'm looking forward to that."

"That's great," said Zaria. "Just be sure to follow up with her. Supervisors tend to forget things like that."

"I will, sis. Thanks for the tip."

When Louis and Justin returned to the room, Justin went to the bathroom to wash his hands, and Louis sat down at the desk.

"Okay, family, let's hit the road," said Louis.

"Dad, it's too early to go to the restaurant," said Jade.

"Well then, I guess I will sit here and relax."

"Dad, I was hoping I could talk to you and mom in private?"

"Sure, baby," said her father. "What is it?"

"Let me go get Justin," said Zaria. "We'll wait for y'all downstairs."

It was time for Jade to tell her parents about Connor. She knew that her parents weren't going to take the news lightly, but she loved

Connor, and she promised him that she would tell her parents the truth about their relationship.

"Well, y'all know Connor is a good friend of mine, right?"

"Yes," her parents said.

"Well, I haven't been completely honest about our friendship. I know I promised not to get involved with anyone while I was in college, and I kept my promise to you for the last three years. But after I met Connor and got to know him, I realized that I liked him, a lot. We started spending a lot of time together, and we eventually started dating."

"Hold the hell up," said her father. "Are you telling us that you and that Connor boy are dating?"

"Yes, Dad."

"How long has this been going on?"

"For about ten months," replied Jade.

Her mother yelled, "Ten months! Isn't that about the time we met him?"

"Not quite," replied Jade. "But that's not important. What's important is that I love him and…"

"Love him," shouted her father.

"In just ten months!" said her mother.

"Mom, you always told me that love is patient and kind, that love always protects and trusts. Connor is all those things to me."

"You should have told us about this a long time ago," said her father.

"I know, Dad. I didn't know how to tell you."

"Jade, I have always told you that you can talk to us about anything. You know that."

"I know, Mom, and I'm sorry for keeping my relationship with Connor from you."

Jade's father took a deep breath and asked, "So how is a long-distance relationship going to work?"

"What do you mean, long-distance relationship?"

"Doesn't Connor live in Georgia? That falls in the long-distance category to me," said her father.

"Well, there is something else I neglected to tell you guys."

"What is it now, Jade? I am about done with all these sudden announcements."

"Connor and I decided to move in together. His parents secured an apartment for us, not too far from my job."

"So that's why Gordon was overly generous with me today. You're their charity case."

"Dad, please," said Jade. "I'm not their charity case. Connor's parents are not like that. They are sweet and kind."

"Jade, you're really trying my patience today," said her father. "Now, how in the hell can y'all afford an apartment?"

"Connor and I have been saving, Dad. We love each other, and we want to start building a life together."

Jade's mother lowered her head. She didn't want to ask the question, but she knew she had to.

She raised her head and asked, "Are you and Connor having sex?"

"Yes," replied Jade.

"There it is," said her father. "You disobeyed us and broke your promise, and now you're having sex. You disappoint me, Jade."

Jade saw the hurt in her parents' eyes. She finally did it. After twenty-one years of making her parents smile, she finally disappointed her parents for the first time in her life.

"I'm sorry for not telling you all this sooner," cried Jade. "But we have been careful. Connor waited until I was ready. And he wanted to be here with me when I told you about our plans."

"Oh really," said her father.

"Yes," said Jade. "I told him that you guys wouldn't like it."

"Well, you're right about that," said her mother. "This was unexpected."

Jade's father stood up and paced the room. Then he asked, "His parents know what's going on between you two?"

"Yes. Connor told his parents months ago, and he thought I had told y'all," replied Jade.

Jade's father stopped pacing and said, "So you have been lying to Connor as well?"

"Yes," replied Jade as she wiped a tear away.

"And you think that's a good way to start a live-in relationship?"

"Absolutely not," cried Jade. "But Connor understood. He loves me."

"And how could you possibly know that after ten months, sweetheart?"

"Because, Dad, Connor looks at me the way you look at Mom, like it's the first time you ever seen her. And when you were sick, it was Connor that made sure I ate, studied, and kept up on my assignments. Isn't that the type of person you want for me?"

"Yes, but later, much later," said her mother. "I'm glad you finally told us. So now that you have other plans, promise us that if you ever need us, for anything, that you will call."

"I promise," said Jade as she gave her mother a kiss.

"I'm going to talk to Connor at dinner," said her father.

"Not at dinner, Dad, please. Can it wait until tomorrow? After we settle in, I'll tell Connor to call you."

"Okay, okay," said her father. "But if Connor doesn't call me, I'll be knocking on your door. Now let's go eat. I'm starving."

4

When Jade and Connor entered their apartment, they breathed in the fresh scent of lavender and vanilla. The place was beautiful. Jade loved how everything fit right into place. Everything was complete with all the fixings.

Jade ran to the back of the apartment where she and Connor would share a bed. She plopped herself on the bed and felt the firm mattress and the fluffy comforter. Jade was in heaven.

Connor stood near the doorway, smiling at Jade's excitement. Connor loved making Jade smile, and he was thrilled that she was happy.

Connor chuckled and said, "My mom said that if there is anything you want changed, just let her know."

"What! Are you kidding? You can't be serious," said Jade. "I love everything about this place. It's perfect, Connor, just perfect."

"Don't you mean almost perfect?"

Jade chuckled.

"Yes, almost perfect," she replied. "All this place needs are pictures of us, and then it will feel like it's really ours."

"I agree," said Connor.

Connor walked over to Jade and sat down next to her and said, "I know we are going to be happy here, Jade. I just know it."

Jade looked into Connor's eyes. They smiled at each other and shared an intimate kiss. Connor got on top of Jade and kissed her ears and neck. Jade was aroused by Connor's touch and she wanted him. She pulled Connor's shirt over his head and caressed his biceps. Connor unbuttoned Jade's shirt, revealing her pink laced bra, and kissed her breasts. Connor loved Jade's sexy body, but her breasts were his favorite. They were the right size, shape, and tenderness. Connor removed Jade's bra, grabbed her breasts, and sucked her nipples.

Connor made his way down to Jade's navel and kissed it. Then he got up on his knees and pulled her shorts and panties off. Jade sat up and pulled down Connor's shorts and briefs. She glanced at his hard penis and smiled.

"The condoms are still packed," whispered Connor.

"I know," said Jade. "Thank God for the pill."

Connor smiled and kissed Jade hard as he entered her. Jade let out a satisfying cry as she wrapped her legs around Connor's body.

"Oh my goodness," said Jade. "You feel so good."

"So do you, baby."

They continued making love, kissing and caressing each other as two people in love do. Connor was gentle and full of pleasure. He made Jade feel special, as if making love to her was a work of art.

After they satisfied each other, Connor held Jade in his arms.

"That was amazing," he said. "And I know we gotta be careful, but I would love to have a baby with you."

"We have time for all that. Let's enjoy us for a while, okay. Oh, by the way, my dad wants to talk to you."

"Oh really. So that's why he was looking at me funny yesterday," said Connor.

"I didn't notice," said Jade. "Please call him later."

"Later as in later today or later this week?"

"Today, Connor."

"Okay, I will," said Connor. "Now let's go raid the fridge, I'm hungry. I'll call your dad after we eat."

"Okay, but I'm gonna take a shower first."

Jade pulled the sheet off Connor, wrapped it around her body and ran into the living room to get her suitcase. She rolled her suitcase into the bedroom and dumped a few items on the bed before she found her nightgown. As Jade neared the bathroom door, she turned around and looked at Connor.

"Are you joining me?" Jade asked as she let the sheet fall to the floor.

Connor leaped from the bed and said, "You bet your sexy ass I am."

After Jade and Connor showered, Jade set the table with their new dinnerware set, and of course, candles. Jade loved candles, especially during romantic evenings like the one she was having with Connor.

Connor warmed up the leftover eggplant and pasta from their graduation dinner. Then he grabbed a bottle of wine out of the small wine cooler and placed it on the table. When the food was ready, Jade made their plates and Connor poured the wine. They held hands, prayed over the food, and enjoyed a romantic dinner together.

"Your mom made this place look beautiful," said Jade. "I'll call her tomorrow to thank her."

"She'll like that," said Connor. "You must have made a good impression on her."

"I guess so," said Jade. "What is your mom trying to do to me?"

"I think she *likes* you as much as I *love* you," said Connor.

"But I only met your mom twice. This is way too much."

"Why would you say that? You know I'm her only child. And like I told you before, my mom has always wanted a daughter. So just embrace it. She's probably not going to let up any time soon," said Connor.

"Are you serious?"

"Very," replied Connor. "You know we're both off tomorrow, so why don't we stay up all night."

"All night. I don't think so, Connor. We gotta finish unpacking, and I have work Tuesday."

"You should have taken my advice and took the whole week off," said Connor.

"True. But it's too late for that now," said Jade.

"It sure is," said Connor.

After dinner, Connor cleaned off the table, and put the dishes in the dishwasher. Jade wiped down the table and the kitchen counters. Then she and Connor cuddled on the couch and watched a movie.

5

Connor's week off from work was beneficial. While Jade worked, Connor unpacked and put their things in the proper places. Afterwards, Connor set up his office in the spare bedroom.

But what Connor liked most about being off for a week was not seeing or hearing from Lisa. Connor thought about Lisa and her annoying phone calls. He was surprised at how quickly she changed from a nice girl to an annoying bitch in just a month.

Connor met Lisa on her first day of work at Ellis Home Solutions when his uncle Greg asked him to show Lisa around the office and train her on the property tracking system. Connor didn't mind at all. He thought Lisa was cute, but he didn't give Lisa any indications that he was interested in her.

The training was scheduled to take two weeks, but Lisa caught on quick and was done with her training in one week. There were a few awkward moments of silence and smiles between them, but Connor was just being Connor.

On the last day of training, Lisa wanted to thank Connor for training her and offered to take him out to lunch. Connor accepted.

After lunch, Connor and Lisa sat in her car and talked about working at EHS.

"So what's it like working for your uncle?" Lisa asked.

"It's cool," replied Connor. "He's not bad."

"Do you get any special treatment?"

"Hell no," said Connor, laughing. "He treats me like a regular employee. If I don't do my job, he'll get on me."

"So what's your story, Connor?" Lisa asked as she stared at him.

"My story?" Connor asked.

"Yeah. Are you married, got a girlfriend, boyfriend?"

"I have a girlfriend," replied Connor.

"I figured that because you're fine as hell," said Lisa.

"Thanks for the compliment," said Connor.

"Look, I know it can be stressful working with family, so if you get stressed out and need a stress reliever, just let me know."

Connor laughed at Lisa's invitation.

"I'm good," he said and jumped out of the car.

The following week, Connor was back to his regular routine. He was a bit surprised at Lisa's daily calls, asking him about the tracking system that she already knew the answers to.

Connor was onto Lisa's game, but he gave her the benefit of the doubt and answered her questions.

Initially, Lisa's calls didn't bother Connor. He was flattered that she wanted to hear his voice. But as the weeks passed, Lisa's conversation changed.

Lisa called Connor and told him all the things she liked to do in bed and how she wanted to do those things with him. Connor was not interested in any of her sexual fantasies. He thought that hanging up on her would work, but it didn't. Every time Connor hung up on Lisa, she called right back or showed up at his cubicle. Eventually, Connor let her calls go to voicemail, and when he could, he avoided Lisa like the plague.

Unfortunately, when Connor returned to work, Lisa picked up where she left off. Lisa called Connor every day, and every day he let her calls go to voicemail.

By Friday afternoon, Connor was fed up. Lisa called Connor three times in one hour, and he was annoyed with her. Connor decided to go to the break room and get a snack. As he was leaving, Lisa entered.

"What's up with you? You can't answer your phone?"

"Lisa, I don't have time for you. And stop calling me!" he replied.

"You're stressed out," said Lisa. "Do you need a stress reliever?"

"No. What I need is for you to stop calling me," replied Connor.

Connor left Lisa in the break room and went back to his desk. He logged off his computer, grabbed his keys, and went home to have a relaxing weekend with Jade.

6

Jade walked into the bathroom and saw a note on the mirror, "*GM, babe, I'm out balling*," signed with a heart. Jade smiled. She jumped in the shower, got dressed, and ate breakfast. She decided that today would be a good day to pick up some decorative frames at Target and get her pictures printed.

As Jade shopped for picture frames, she picked up a few bath towels, wash rags, and sexy panties. She made sure to pick up a few blue towels as well. Connor's favorite color was blue, and he would appreciate Jade thinking of him.

"Hey, baby. Where are you?"

"Target. What's up?"

"Nothing. I just got back from playing ball with Nelson. We chillin' at the house."

"Don't y'all sit y'all sweaty asses on my couch," joked Jade.

"Too late." Connor laughed. "Can you pick up some Gatorade?"

"What flavor?"

"Any flavor will do," replied Connor.

"Okay. I'll see you in a few. Love you," said Jade.

"Love you too," said Connor.

Jade hung up and continued shopping. When she was done, she made her way to the register, checked out, and went home.

Jade dropped her keys on the table as she entered the apartment. When she entered the kitchen, she saw Connor searching for something to eat in the fridge and Nelson sitting at the table, drinking a glass of water.

"Hey, guys. What's up?"

"Hey, sweetie. Nothing, just hungry," said Connor.

"I think there's some tuna salad on the top shelf," said Jade.

"Found it," said Connor. "You want some, man?"

"Nah, I'm good," replied Nelson.

"Oh, here's your Gatorade," said Jade as she gave Connor a kiss.

"Thanks, baby."

"How are you doing, Nelson?"

"Good," replied Nelson. "How have you been?"

"Great! How was the game?" Jade asked.

"You know it was on," said Nelson. "Connor's getting rather good too. I wish he would play more often."

"Nelson, man, you know I'm busy," said Connor.

"Whatever. Ain't nobody that damn busy." Nelson laughed.

"I'll be right back," said Jade.

"Okay, baby," said Connor.

Jade went to the bedroom and emptied her bags. She pulled the tags off her new items and threw everything into the washing machine.

"Baby, I'm gonna take a shower," said Connor.

"Okay, I'll go keep Nelson company," said Jade.

Jade returned to the kitchen and saw Connor's empty plate on the table. She huffed and said, "He never puts his plate in the sink."

Nelson chuckled and took a gulp of his water. "You want some more water, Nelson?"

"Sure," replied Nelson.

Jade grabbed the empty glass and filled it with water. She turned around and looked at Nelson, who was staring at her.

"What?" Jade asked curiously.

"Nothing," replied Nelson.

"Why are you staring at me?"

"My bad," replied Nelson. "I was daydreaming."

"And what exactly were you daydreaming about?" Jade asked as she set the glass of water on the table.

"Lots of things," replied Nelson.

"Do tell," said Jade.

Jade was anxious to hear what Nelson had on his mind. Nelson always had good conversation, and Jade enjoyed talking to him. As Nelson was about to disclose his daydreaming fantasies, Connor conveniently interrupted them.

"What are y'all talking about?" Connor asked.

"Nothing," replied Nelson. "What took you so long?"

"Sorry, man, but that shower felt good. Only one thing was missing," Connor said, as he blew Jade a kiss.

Nelson looked at Jade and saw the same smile that melted his heart when he first saw her. The same smile that he hoped to put on her face one day.

Nelson's thoughts went back to the night when he first saw Jade. *It was at Club Paradise, and Nelson thought he had just seen an angel. When Nelson saw her at the bar, ordering a drink, he was in awe. Who was she? Nelson thought. She was gorgeous! Nelson wanted to approach her, but some guy was flirting with her, and when Nelson saw her smile, he smiled. Later, when Nelson went searching for her, she was dancing with his best friend, Connor.*

"You two are too much," said Nelson.

"Ah, man, don't hate. You'll find someone special one day too."

"That's true," said Jade. "There's someone out there for you."

"I'm sure there is, but I like the single life," said Nelson.

"Well, how do you feel about Sophie or Becca?" Jade asked. "You know I can hook that up for you."

"Not interested," replied Nelson.

Jade and Connor laughed.

"Guys, I'm gonna go home and get out of these sweaty clothes. C, we gotta hang out more. Jade, as always, it's good to see you. I would give you a hug, but…"

"I know." Jade laughed. "I'll take a raincheck."

"Yo, Nelson, don't forget the dinner party next month."

"It's on my calendar," said Nelson. "See y'all later."

Connor let Nelson out and then joined Jade in the family room where she was organizing their pictures and figuring out which picture looked best in which frame.

"Can I help?" Connor asked.

"Sure," replied Jade.

"For one, I don't think you have enough frames for all these pictures," said Connor.

"I know." Jade chuckled. "We'll have to work with what we got for now."

As Connor sat down to help Jade, his phone rang. He wondered who was calling him on a Saturday afternoon. He looked at his phone but didn't recognize the number.

"Excuse me, baby, let me answer this," he said.

"I hope that's not the office," said Jade as Connor walked out of the room.

"Hello," said Connor.

"Hey, it's Lisa."

"How did you get my number, and why are you calling me?"

"I got your number from the office roster, duh. And I'm calling you because you don't answer my calls at work."

"Look, Lisa. There is absolutely no reason for you to call me on my cell. You know I have a girlfriend. Don't call me again!"

Connor hung up and went back into the family room.

"Do you have to go into the office?" Jade asked.

"Nope," replied Connor.

Connor seemed a bit agitated from the call, and Jade noticed.

"Is everything okay?" Jade asked.

"Yeah," replied Connor.

Connor hoped everything was okay. And he hoped Lisa got the message.

"So what do you think?"

"I think you did a great job without me," said Connor.

"Thanks. Now we can put them up. Then, I'm going to put on something nice so you can take me to the movies."

"Sounds good to me. What do you wanna see?"

"*The Shallows*," replied Jade.

31

Jade and Connor put the pictures up. She was pleased with their work. Jade went to the bedroom and put on her skinny jeans and a cute shirt. She put her hair up in a ponytail and put a little makeup on. She was ready to go.

"You look mad sexy in those jeans, girl."

"Thanks," said Jade. "Your cologne smells good. Who are you wearing?"

"Hugo Boss. It's my favorite," said Connor.

"I like when you wear that Lagerfeld. It turns me on," said Jade.

"Well, I can go put that on, and then we can have a little fun before we go." Connor laughed.

"Boy, I'll miss the movie, messing with you. Let's go." Jade laughed.

Connor and Jade held hands as he drove to the movie theater. Jade put her Beyoncé CD into the CD player and they sang along to the music. Neither one of them could sing, but to them, they sounded wonderful.

When they reached the mall, Connor parked the car, and he and Jade walked hand in hand into the movie theater. As soon as they got in line to purchase their tickets, a sweet elderly woman turned around and struck up a conversation with Connor.

"How long you two been married?"

"Excuse me?" said Connor.

"How long you been married, boy?" she repeated. "You deaf or something?"

"Oh, no, ma'am. We're not married," replied Connor.

The elderly woman asked, "Well, whatcha waiting for? I can see that you love her."

"Yes, I do," said Connor.

The elderly woman asked again, "Well then, whatcha waiting for?"

Connor laughed and said, "I think your friends are waiting on you, ma'am."

"Oh darn," she said. "They always in a rush. Rush, rush, rush."

"Have a good evening and enjoy your movie," said Connor.

* * *

On the way home, Jade called Vinny's and placed a to-go order.

"Our food will be ready in twenty minutes," said Jade.

"Cool. So how did you like the movie?" Connor asked.

"I liked it," replied Jade. "Now do you see why I don't do beaches?"

"What! I don't think there are sharks in the Virginia beaches, Jade."

"Yeah, whatever. I'm still not going too far in that water."

"You're a trip." Connor laughed. "What about that old lady? She looked like she was about to hit me with her cane," said Connor.

"Oh man, she was funny...asking that silly question," said Jade.

"What do you mean, silly question?"

"We are too young to get married," replied Jade. "Plus, I'm not ready to get married."

"So are you saying that if I ask you to marry me, this very minute, you would say no?"

"Yep," replied Jade jokingly.

"Damn girl, that's cold." Connor chuckled.

Connor parked in front of Vinny's and gave Jade his credit card. Jade jumped out of the BMW and went inside the restaurant. As Jade approached the counter, she was met by a tall handsome guy.

The tall handsome guy looked at Jade and said, "Hello. How can I help you?"

"Hi. I called in a shrimp scampi," said Jade.

"Oh yes," he said. "It will be right up, miss."

"Thank you. Are you new?" Jade asked. "I haven't seen you here before. Where's Vinny?"

The tall handsome guy laughed at Jade's innocent inquiries.

"No, ma'am, I'm not," he replied. "I work at another location across town, and Vinny is on vacation."

"Oh yeah, that's right," said Jade. "I completely forgot. I hope he's having a good time."

He smiled at Jade and asked, "You live around here?"

"Uh, no. Just passing through," replied Jade with a puzzled look on her face.

"My bad. I didn't mean to get in your business. Just trying to make conversation," he said with a smile.

Jade noticed he had a nice smile. She also noticed his braids. They were on point.

"One shrimp scampi. That'll be twenty dollars," he said. "How would you like to pay for that, ma'am?"

"Debit please," replied Jade.

"No problem. Go ahead and swipe," he said as he smiled at Jade.

"Mmm! That smells good," said Jade. "Thank you."

"You're welcome. Enjoy your dinner and come back to see us."

Jade smiled and walked out of the restaurant. She jumped in the car and placed the food on the back seat.

"That smells delicious," said Connor.

"It sure does, and I can't wait to get home and eat," said Jade. "Do we have any wine left?"

"We sure do," replied Connor.

As Connor entered the parking garage, the word *unknown* popped up on his Bluetooth. Connor knew Jade saw it, and he knew he would have some explaining to do. Connor looked over at Jade, but he didn't say anything to her.

When they entered the apartment, Jade went into the kitchen to set the table. In silence she grabbed two plates and two wine glasses out of the cabinet and set them on the counter. Connor took the shrimp scampi out of the bag and made their plates. He grabbed two forks out of the drawer, got the wine, and filled their glasses. When they sat down at the table, Connor grasped Jade's hand.

"I know you're wondering about the calls," said Connor. "That was Lisa, from the office."

"Lisa. Who is she and why is she calling you on your cell?"

"She's the new girl, and I don't know why she's calling me," replied Connor.

But Connor did know. He didn't want to lie to Jade, but he felt he had to. There was no way for Connor to explain to Jade why Lisa was calling him without it leading to more questions.

"Does she know you have a girlfriend?"

"Yes," replied Connor.

"Well then, I guess we don't have anything to worry about," said Jade.

"We don't," Connor said matter-of-factly as he squeezed Jade's hand. "Because for one, I love you and only you. And two, she doesn't compare to you…in any way, Jade. I'll take care of it Monday."

* * *

When Connor arrived at work, his priority was to talk to Lisa. He walked over to Lisa's cubicle, but she wasn't at her desk. Connor went back to his desk and logged on to his computer. He made a couple of calls and set up a few appointments to go out in the field.

After that, he checked the property database and sent e-mails to his team members. Then Connor went to his ten o'clock team leader meeting. An hour later, the meeting was over. When Connor walked out of the conference room, he saw Lisa talking to Deanna.

"Excuse me, ladies," said Connor. "Lisa, can I talk to you for a minute."

"Sure," said Lisa.

Lisa followed Connor into the conference room and sat down. Connor moved a few feet away from Lisa and sat on the edge of the table.

"You like my dress, Connor? I wore it just for you. Everything I wear is for you, Connor."

"Look, Lisa, calling me on my cell is inappropriate," said Connor. "And I already told you to stop calling me."

"What the hell is wrong with you?" Lisa asked with an attitude.

"Are you serious? You called me on my cell, twice," said Connor. "And you're asking me what's wrong? What the hell is wrong with you? How many times do I have to tell you to stop calling me? You and I are not going to happen."

"That's what you think," said Lisa.

Lisa stood up, winked at Connor, and walked out of the conference room.

7

Jade spent most of the day getting ready for her dinner party. She was excited to be hosting a party and wanted everything to be picture-perfect. She cleaned the bathrooms, vacuumed, and mopped the kitchen floor. Connor helped by dusting the furniture and setting the dining room table. Their apartment looked great.

Jade opened the windows to let some fresh air in. She liked the way the sun cascaded through the windows and into the apartment. She lit a few candles to allow the aroma to fill the room. Connor opened the French doors and stepped onto the balcony. He enjoyed sitting on the balcony and taking in the fresh air. Although Connor wished for a beach view, the view of the neighborhood park was satisfying.

"Come sit down with me for a minute," yelled Connor.

"Baby, we gotta get dressed," said Jade. "Our guests will be here soon."

"We got a good thirty minutes to relax. C'mon, Jade. Take a little breather with me, please," whined Connor.

"Okay, I'm coming," said Jade.

Jade grabbed two bottles of water out of the fridge and joined Connor on the balcony. The breeze felt good. She and Connor watched the kids as they played in the park. The thought of playing in the park with Connor and their kids made Jade smile.

"What are you smiling about?" Connor asked.

"Those kids," replied Jade. "They're fearless. Jumping off the swings like that, I'm amazed."

"They're having a good time," said Connor.

"Yes, they are," said Jade.

"So what's on the menu?"

"You'll see," replied Jade. "I found some great dinner party recipes online. I just hope everything tastes good." Jade laughed.

"Well, it sure smells good in there," said Connor. "I can't wait to eat dinner and you know what else."

"Boy, quit it," said Jade. "Let's go get ready before we get in trouble and miss our own dinner party."

Connor and Jade got dressed and waited patiently for their friends to arrive. Jade checked on the food, and Connor put the hors d'oeuvres on the table.

"Baby, that was the doorbell. Can you get it? It should be Sophia and Becca."

"I'm on it," replied Connor.

Connor opened the door, and to his surprise, stood Nelson and Marcus.

"Hey, fellas, what's up?" Connor asked. "I'm glad y'all made it. And you come bearing gifts."

Connor hugged his friends and led them into the family room.

"Yo, C, this crib is nice," said Marcus.

"Thanks. Make yourselves at home," said Connor.

"This is for you and Jade," said Nelson as he handed Connor a gift. "So make sure you open it with her. Where is she anyway?"

"In the kitchen, checking on the food," replied Connor. "What are y'all drinking?"

"Rum and coke for me," replied Nelson.

"I'll have a beer," replied Marcus.

"Coming right up," said Connor. Connor went to the kitchen to get their drinks.

"That was Nelson and Marcus," said Connor as he stepped into the kitchen.

"Oh, cool. Let me go say hello," said Jade.

"Oh my goodness, y'all made it," said Jade as she stepped into the family room. "It's so good to see y'all."

Jade walked toward Marcus, opened her arms, and gave him a hug.

"Looking good, Marcus," she said.

"Thanks," said Marcus. "You too, Jade. This place is nice. I like the decor."

"Thanks, Marcus, but I must give credit to Connor's mom, she did all of it. Isn't it lovely?"

"Yes, it is," replied Marcus.

"This place isn't the only thing that's lovely," said Nelson.

"Aww, thanks," said Jade. "Come over here and give me my raincheck."

Nelson looked Jade up and down as he walked toward her. He planted a kiss on her cheek and gave her a hug.

"You look beautiful," he whispered. "I keep thinking about the last time I saw you, and..."

"One rum and coke for you, and one cold beer for you," said Connor as he handed his buddies their drinks.

"I guess I'll tell you later," said Nelson.

"Where are Sophie and Becca?" Marcus asked.

"They're on their way," replied Jade. "Becca just texted me. They made a pit stop."

"Cool. Now where is the bathroom?" Marcus laughed.

"You gotta take a piss already, man," said Connor. "Damn. It's right down the hall, first door on the right."

"Thanks, man. Be right back," said Marcus.

"Baby, did you show Nelson the view from the balcony yet?"

"No, he didn't," replied Nelson sarcastically.

"Well, you gotta see it," said Jade. "It's nice."

Jade smiled at Nelson. Nelson tried hard not to stare at Jade, but she looked stunning in her pink-and-green floral summer dress. It fit her body perfectly, and Nelson liked what he saw.

"Okay, c'mon, I'll show you the view," said Connor.

Jade jumped up with excitement when she heard the doorbell. "That must be my girls," she said.

"Coming," yelled Jade.

When Jade opened the door, she saw Sophia and Becca standing in the doorway. Jade opened her arms and hugged Sophia and Becca at the same time. After the exchange of hugs and kisses, Jade led Sophia and Becca into the family room.

"Wow, this is huge," said Sophia. "Who the heck lives here besides you and Connor?"

Jade laughed and replied, "Just us two. Isn't the space wonderful?"

"Yes, it is," replied Sophia. "I love it. Where's Connor?"

"On the balcony with Nelson," replied Jade.

"Oh. Well, here's a small gift from us to you," said Sophia. "We hope you like it."

"I'm sure I will. You girls always give me nice things," said Jade.

"Y'all want something to drink?" Jade asked as she placed her gift on the sofa table.

"Nah, we're good," replied Becca.

"Oh, here's Marcus," said Jade. "He was just asking about y'all."

Marcus smiled when he saw Sophia and Becca and greeted them with hugs and kisses. Then he picked up his beer and sat down near the fireplace.

Connor and Nelson made their way back inside the house and joined their friends in the family room.

"How are you two lovely ladies doing this evening?" Connor asked.

"We're doing well," replied Becca as she gave Connor a hug.

"Y'all still looking good, I see," said Connor.

"No doubt," said Sophia as she hugged Connor.

"Now where's my hug?" Nelson asked.

Sophia and Becca laughed before they gave Nelson a hug.

Jade adored her friends. Each one of them were special to her. Whenever Jade and her friends hung out either at the bar, a club, or a restaurant, they always had fun.

Nelson was the brainiac of the group and always had an interesting conversation to share. But Nelson also liked to joke and have fun. Jade liked that about Nelson because he always made her laugh.

Sophia was very much into herself, but in a good way. She was beautiful and attracted a lot of guys because of her exotic features. By no means was Sophia conceited; she just liked to look good.

Marcus was the serious one in the group. Everything had to be planned with Marcus. Jade would often tell Marcus to lighten up and stop being so serious. But Marcus was Marcus and stuck to his structured lifestyle.

Becca was cute and had a baby face. She was laid-back and enjoyed staying home most of the time. Jade liked being around Becca because Becca had positive vibes. Becca looked at the good in every bad situation and always had good advice to share.

"Okay, family," yelled Jade. "Let's make our way into the dining room. Time for the appetizers."

"What are we having?" Marcus asked.

"You'll see," replied Connor.

Jade, Connor, and their friends went into the dining room. Connor grabbed two bottles of wine out of the cooler and placed them on the table before he took his seat.

After Jade lit the candles, she went to the kitchen to get the shrimp cocktail. Six large shrimp cocktails were placed neatly on a serving tray ready to be served. Jade placed a shrimp cocktail in front of each of her friends.

"These shrimps are huge," said Marcus.

"You better believe it," said Connor. "Only the best for our friends. Wait until you see the main course."

"Whatever it is, it sure smells good," said Nelson.

"Thanks. Now eat up," said Jade.

Jade and her friends ate their shrimp cocktail and drank wine as music played in the background. After the appetizers, Jade prepared the dinner plates, and Connor refilled the wine glasses.

"You put your foot in this chicken parmesan," said Nelson.

"I agree," said Becca. "This is delicious."

"Thanks, guys," said Jade.

"So what did your parents think about this setup?" Sophie asked.

"They weren't too happy, especially hearing all about it at graduation," replied Jade.

"You told your parents about all this on graduation day!" Becca asked. "Are you insane!"

"I know, I know," replied Jade. "I procrastinate. But I think everything is okay now. Connor spoke to my dad, and I think he set my dad at ease."

"What do you mean, you *think*?" Becca asked.

"Well, Connor didn't tell me what they talked about, Becca. He only told me that my dad was okay with us living together."

"And he'll probably never tell you," added Sophia. "Connor's smart. Plus, you're twenty-one, and it's your life, so you can do whatever you want."

"You can say that again," added Becca.

"I hear y'all, but you know how my parents are," said Jade. "You should have seen their faces when I broke the news to them. They were so disappointed. My parents didn't call me for a week. I had to call them, and when I did, they barely had anything to say to me. Thank God they're finally coming around."

"Girl, your parents are going to be fine," said Sophia. "Tonight we are celebrating a new chapter in your life. You and Connor together, being happy."

"I'll drink to that," said Jade as she lifted her glass.

"What are y'all toasting to?" Nelson asked.

"The next chapter of Jade and Connor's happiness," replied Sophia.

"Well then, let me add something," said Nelson. "To my boy C and his boo. May you both continue to love each other and enjoy your new place. And most of all, give me some nieces and nephews before I'm thirty." Nelson laughed.

"Now, I will surely drink to that," yelled Connor as he winked at Jade.

"You're a hot mess, Nelson," said Jade.

After Jade and her friends cleaned the kitchen, they joined the guys in the family room.

Connor found one of his party playlists and turned up the volume. He grabbed Jade's hands and danced with her. His friends followed. Marcus danced with Sophia, and Nelson danced with Becca.

"I see you still got moves for a white guy, Connor," said Sophia.

"Girl, I'm Black and Italian," replied Connor. "And yes, I still got 'em."

After a few fast songs, Connor wanted to slow dance with Jade.

"Can we get the floor, y'all?" Connor asked as he stared at Jade.

"Absolutely," said Sophia.

"Man, y'all can do that later," said Nelson.

"Boy, sit down and let Connor do his thing," said Marcus.

Connor played Monica's "Why I Love You So Much," for Jade.

"That's my favorite song," said Jade.

"I know," said Connor. Connor grabbed Jade's hands, spun her around, and slow danced with her.

Becca and Marcus went out to the balcony. Sophia and Nelson sat down and watched Jade and Connor dance. Nelson stared at Jade and admired how the flicker of the candles made her face glow.

Sophia noticed how attentive Nelson was as he watched Connor dance with Jade. She looked deeper at Nelson and noticed that his eyes were glued on Jade. He had that look, and Sophia knew what it was. Nelson was in love with Jade.

As the evening passed, Jade and her friends played spades, taboo, and charades. And of course, nothing was better than having the girls against the guys in charades. As the night came to an end, Jade and Connor thanked their friends for coming and wished them a good night.

"You did a great job," said Connor.

"We did a great job, and I appreciate all your help," said Jade.

Connor walked over to Jade and grabbed her hands and said, "Now let's go to bed. I want you so bad tonight."

"In a minute, baby. I want to upload my pictures first."

As Jade was uploading the pictures, her phone rang.

"Hey, Jade."

"Hey, Sophie. What's up?"

"Sorry to call so late, but how well do you know Nelson?"

"How well? I don't know." Jade laughed. "I've known him for almost a year. Why? Do you like him?"

"Nah, girl," replied Sophia. "He's not my type."

"Okay, so why are you asking me about him, Sophie?"

"Well, when you and Connor were slow dancing, I noticed Nelson staring at you, hard," replied Sophia.

"Funny you mentioned that," said Jade. "When Nelson was here a few weeks ago, I caught him staring at me, and he said he was daydreaming."

"Well, his stare didn't look like he was daydreaming to me," said Sophia. "He was staring at you like he wanted you. Now, I like Nelson, but I don't know him that well, so be careful."

"Nelson is harmless, Sophie."

"Just be careful, please," begged Sophia.

"Okay, girl," said Jade. "Oh, I have something to tell you and Becca."

"What is it?" Sophia asked.

"I need to tell y'all in person," replied Jade. "Let's meet up at Vinny's next Saturday at one."

"Sounds good. I'll let Becca know. Later, Jade."

"Good night, Sophie."

Jade hung up and finished uploading her pictures. Connor blew out the candles and turned down the lights.

"Was that Sophie?"

"Yes," replied Jade. "She said that Nelson was watching us slow dance. Does that seem weird to you?"

"No. Nelson was probably just trying to steal some of my moves," replied Connor.

"Whatever." Jade laughed.

Jade put her phone on silent. She walked up to Connor and wrapped her arms around his waist.

"Let's go to bed now," she whispered. "I want you too."

"That's what I like to hear," said Connor.

Connor touched Jade's face and gave her a passionate tongue kiss. He picked her up and carried her into the bedroom. In the bedroom, Connor pulled off her dress and threw it on the floor. Jade undid her bra and took off her panties. Connor quickly took off his clothes and threw them on the floor. They got in the bed, and Connor climbed on top of Jade. He was ready to satisfy her. Jade felt Connor's hard penis against her body and wanted to feel him inside her.

Connor kissed Jade on her lips before he moved to her neck. Then he kissed her breasts. Connor took his time. He grabbed each breast, one by one, and sucked her nipples until they got hard.

He made his way down to Jade's stomach and kissed her navel. Then he gently opened Jade's legs and kissed the inside of her thighs.

Connor licked the outer parts of Jade's vagina. Jade moaned as she ran her fingers through his hair. Jade enjoyed what Connor was doing to her. And when Connor put his tongue inside her vagina, she let out a loud, satisfying sigh.

"Oh my goodness, that feels so good," whispered Jade. "Don't stop. Keep going, baby, keep going."

As Connor caressed Jade's breasts with his free hand, he moved his tongue deeper inside her. Her moans got louder and louder as she felt the intensity of Connor's tongue inside her.

"Oh my goodness, I'm about to cum."

Connor braced himself to accept Jade's juices. As Jade relieved herself, she let out a satisfying cry. Connor had pleased her.

Jade woke up to the smell of fresh coffee, bacon, eggs, and biscuits. She was surprised Connor wasn't out on his Saturday run. But today Jade didn't care either way. It was Saturday, and it was her day to treat herself to her monthly salon visit. Afterward Jade had plans to meet Sophia and Becca for lunch at Vinny's.

Connor was taking the biscuits out of the oven when Jade walked into the kitchen. Jade smiled as she admired how sexy Connor looked in his briefs. She snuck up behind him and grabbed his butt cheek.

"Hey," yelled Connor. "What are you doing? You almost made me drop the biscuits."

"Sorry, but I couldn't resist," said Jade, laughing. "No run today?"

"Nope," replied Connor. "I'm gonna meet up with Nelson and shoot some hoops."

"Okay. I'll be at the salon, and then I'm having lunch with my girls."

"Cool," said Connor.

Jade grabbed two coffee mugs out of the cabinet and poured the coffee into the mugs. Connor liked his coffee black. Jade detested black coffee. She liked cream and sugar in hers. Connor grabbed their plates off the island, and he and Jade sat down in the family room and ate breakfast together.

"Good job on breakfast," said Jade. "That hit the spot."

"Filled you up, huh?"

"Sure did," replied Jade.

"Oh, before I forget. I gotta go to Charlotte for work," said Connor.

"Charlotte. When?"

"The week after the fourth of July," replied Connor.

"For how long?"

"Just a couple of days," replied Connor. "You should have Sophia and Becca come over and stay with you."

"No way," said Jade. "I'm looking forward to having the place to myself."

Connor laughed and said, "You're too much, girl."

"So are we still going to your parents' house for the fourth?"

"Of course," replied Connor. "My mom is looking forward to seeing you again and showing you off to my family."

"Can't wait for that," said Jade as she rolled her eyes. "I'm gonna go get dressed. I got a long day."

Jade went to the bedroom and got dressed. She put on a cute coral summer dress and added a little makeup and eyeshadow. In her accessory drawer, she found her white bandanna and wrapped it around the top of her head and allowed her hair to hang down her back. Then Jade grabbed her coral sandals out of the closet and put them on. She was ready to go.

"Okay, baby, I'm out," said Jade as she gave Connor a kiss. "Can you make the bed before you leave?"

"You look cute," said Connor. "All that for the salon?"

Jade laughed and replied, "You know how me and my girls do. Don't forget to make the bed, sweetie."

"Okay, okay, see you later," said Connor. "Have fun."

"You too," said Jade. "Oh, I almost forgot. I need some money."

"Ah, man. I forgot to stop at the bank yesterday. Just take my card, Jade. It's in my wallet."

"You're not going to need it today?"

"Nope. I have a little cash on me," replied Connor.

"Okay. Thanks," said Jade. "See you later."

"Uh-huh," mumbled Connor as he watched *Fixer Upper*.

* * *

Jade was a few minutes late for her appointment. Lucky for Jade, Alexa was still working on a client when she arrived.

"Hey, Ms. Jade. How are you doing?" Alexa asked.

"Good," replied Jade. "Sorry I'm late."

"It's okay," said Alexa. "I'll be ready for you in a minute."

Jade sat down and looked in a *Black Hair* magazine while she waited. She hoped to find a cute but simple hairdo that would keep her from doing her hair while she was in Georgia.

"Okay, Jade, I'm ready," yelled Alexa.

Jade put the magazine down on the table and walked over to Alexa's booth.

"You look cute and glowy today," said Alexa.

"She's either in love or pregnant," said one of the beauticians.

Jade laughed and said, "It's definitely love because I am not pregnant."

"Did you find anything in the mag?" Alexa asked.

"Sure did," replied Jade. "I like those locked twists with the hair out."

"Ooh, I like," said Alexa. "I got you."

Four hours later, Jade's hair, nails, and toes were done. She paid for the services and thanked her beauticians for making her look beautiful.

It was almost one o'clock by the time Jade left the salon. "There's no way I'm gonna make it to Vinny's by one," said Jade as she started her car. Before Jade pulled out of the parking lot, she called Sophia.

"Hey, Sophie. I'm heading to Vinny's now. The salon took longer than I expected."

"Okay. We're parking now," said Sophia. "We'll go inside and get a booth. See you soon, girl."

"Okay," said Jade.

Jade turned on the radio and sped up. "All this damn traffic," she said to herself. "C'mon, people, move out of my way." Jade sung along to the music until she was interrupted by a call from Connor.

"Are you still at the salon?"

"Nope. Just left," replied Jade. "I'm heading to Vinny's now."

"Oh, okay. I'm gonna hang out at Nelson's after we shoot hoops, so I'll see you later tonight, okay."

"Okay," said Jade. "I'll try and wait up for you."

"*Ti amo,*" said Connor.

Jade found a parking spot in the rear of Vinny's. She parked and went inside the restaurant. Jade stood near the door and looked around. She didn't see Sophia or Becca anywhere. When a small group of kids moved out of Jade's view, she saw Sophia and Becca sitting in the booth. Jade waved her hand and walked over to the booth.

"Hey," said Jade as she sat down next to Becca. "I made it."

"You're late," joked Becca.

"Sorry. I got there late, and the salon was crowded. I guess everybody is getting ready for the fourth of July."

"I see Alexa hooked you up again," said Sophia. "I might have to go see her. Does she do sew-ins?"

"She does everything, Sophie," replied Jade.

"We ordered you a sweet tea," said Becca.

"Thanks," said Jade.

Jade looked at the menu. She wanted something other than her usual shrimp scampi.

"What are y'all getting?" Jade asked.

"We have no idea," replied Sophie.

"Well, I'm going to get the shrimp carbonara," said Jade.

"Now that sounds delicious," said Becca.

As Jade put her menu down, a tall guy walked over to their table, holding a tray with three cups of water on it.

"So you came back," he said as he looked at Jade.

His deep voice got Becca's attention. His caramel complexion and facial features were a perfect combination. His cornrows were flawless, and his smile was to die for.

Becca's eyes were glued on the tall guy, but his eyes were glued on Jade. He stared at Jade as he placed the cups on the table.

"I was wondering when you were coming back," he said as he tucked the tray under his arm.

"Excuse me?" said Jade.

"You're the shrimp scampi girl, right?"

"How do you remember that?" Jade asked.

"I never forget a pretty face," he replied. "What's your name?"

"Her name is Jade, and she has a man," replied Sophia. "Are you ready to take our orders or what?"

"No, ma'am. I'm not the waiter," he replied. "But since I'm here, I'll go ahead and take your orders for y'all."

"That's nice of you," said Jade. "Thank you."

The handsome guy smiled at Jade and took their orders. As he made his way back to the kitchen, he turned around and winked at Jade.

"Who was that, Jade?" Becca asked. "He is fine."

"I don't know," replied Jade. "And Sophie, that was rude."

"Bitch, please, I'm hungry." Sophie laughed. "So what's up? What do you have to tell us?"

"I think Connor is cheating on me with one of his coworkers."

"What makes you think that?" Sophia asked.

"Because the bitch called him on his cell," replied Jade.

"What! How do you know that?" Becca asked.

"Because I was with Connor when she called, Becca. I was mad as hell, but I kept my cool."

"So what did Connor say?" Sophia asked.

"That she was a new employee and that he would take care of it."

"Well, you know how Connor is," said Sophia. "If he said he'll take care of it, then he'll take care of it."

"Yeah, but they work together, like every day, Sophie. How do I know if he took care of it? They could be having some office romance and shit behind my back."

"Jade, honestly, I can't comprehend it," said Sophia. "Connor loves you. Don't get yourself all worked up over nothing. There is no way he's cheating. But if I find out that he is, I will kick his Italian ass, and then find that bitch and kick her ass too."

"I agree with Sophie, Jade. I have never seen anyone love the way Connor loves you. You both give me hope that true love is out there, and one day, I hope I find it too."

"But he's human," said Jade. "And what if I give him my all, and—"

Sophia stopped Jade from talking. She reached across the table and touched Jade's hand.

"Do you love Connor?" Sophia asked.

"With every fiber of my being," replied Jade.

"Then why are you letting this bother you? Talk to Connor about it and let him know how you feel."

"Now that's something Becca would say," said Jade.

"I know, right," said Becca. "But I totally agree with Sophie."

"You girls are awesome," said Jade.

As Jade dabbed her eyes, a thick-sized girl stopped at their table with two plates of food on the sleeve of her arm and one plate in her left hand.

"Okay, ladies, time to get your grub on," she said. "Who gets the spaghetti and meatballs?"

"I do," said Becca. "Thanks."

"Who gets the shrimp po-boy with fries?"

"That would be mine," said Sophia.

"And I guess the shrimp carbonara is yours," she said.

"Yes, thank you," said Jade.

"You're welcome, ladies. Let me know if you need anything else."

"Wait, hold up," said Sophia. "Who's the tall, handsome brother with the braids?"

"Oh, you must be talking about Renz," replied the waitress. "Isn't he a hottie? The young girls love him. Always running in here to buy a soda just to see him. It's crazy."

"Well, he *is* fine," said Becca. "What kind of name is Renz?"

"His name is Lorenzo, but we call him Renz," she replied. "Do you need to see him?"

"Nah," replied Sophia. "Thanks."

The waitress smiled at Sophia and walked away.

Before Jade started eating, she took a picture of her food and sent it to Connor.

A few minutes later, the waitress returned.

"How are we doing, ladies?" she asked as she refilled their drinks.

"Good," replied Sophia. "Can we get the checks please?"

"Sure," replied the waitress. "One check or separate checks?"

The girls looked at each other and laughed. "Separate," they replied.

"No problem, ladies. Be right back."

Jade watched the waitress walk over to a table where two adults and a little girl were sitting. The little girl looked about three years old, and she was cute as a button. Jade smiled and thought about what the beautician said. She hoped that she would have Connor's child one day, but not now. Jade still had too much to do in her life, and she was nowhere near ready for a child.

"Excuse me, ladies," said the tall guy. "My girl got busy, so here are your checks. You can pay at the counter when you're ready."

"Thanks, Renz," said Becca in a flirtatious voice.

Renz smiled at Becca and walked away.

"See what I mean," said Jade. "He stares and smiles at us, and he got a girl. Men are a trip. Let's go!"

Jade and her friends walked up to the counter to pay for their food. A young lady took care of Becca, then Sophia. As Jade stepped to the counter to pay, Renz told the young lady to take a break.

"So your name is Jade, huh?" Renz asked.

"Yes, it is," replied Jade.

"That's a nice name. I'm Renz."

"I know," said Jade.

"Let me take care of that for you," he said.

"What do you mean?"

"Your tab. I got it," replied Renz.

"No, no, I am perfectly capable of paying my own tab," said Jade.

"I'm sure you are, but today, your lunch is on me," said Renz. "You must live a pretty distance away, huh?"

"Excuse me?" said Jade.

"Well, I thought you would have been back sooner than today," said Renz. "Wishful thinking, I guess."

"Listen, I gotta go," said Jade. "My friends are waiting."

"When will you be back?" Renz asked. "I want to make sure I'm here."

"I have a boyfriend," replied Jade. "And if I do come back, it's because I love the food here, not because I want to see you."

"Ouch!" said Renz as he placed his hand over his heart. "By the way, you are gorgeous!"

"Thanks for my lunch. I really appreciate it," said Jade.

Jade hurried out of the restaurant and met Sophia and Becca outside.

"Was something wrong with your check?" Sophia asked.

"No," replied Jade. "Renz had the nerve to ask me when I was coming back."

"What did you tell him?" Becca asked.

"I reminded him that I have a boyfriend." Jade laughed.

"Maybe I should go back in there," said Becca.

"For what?" said Jade. "He's a player." She chuckled. "I'll see y'all later."

Jade and her friends exchanged hugs and kisses before leaving Vinny's. As she drove home, she thought about the conversation she had with Sophia and Becca. Her friends were right about Connor. Connor loved Jade. Jade felt Connor's love every time he looked at her, every time he kissed her, and every time he made love to her.

But Jade also knew that no one was perfect. And no matter how much a guy loves his girl or how beautiful she may be, some men get weak and fall prey to the pussy.

Jade thought about Lisa and wondered what she looked like. She thought about how close their cubicles were at work and if Lisa and Connor talked to each other throughout the day. Jade hated having such thoughts, but she couldn't help but wonder if there was something going on between Connor and Lisa. Jade decided to take Sophia's advice and talk to Connor about the situation.

9

The basketball courts were crowded by the time Connor and Nelson arrived. Spectators sat in the bleachers, clapping their hands and screaming obscenities at the players. Connor and Nelson walked to the far end of the court and put their duffel bags on the bench.

"We got next," yelled Nelson.

Connor and Nelson sat down on the bleachers and patiently waited for their turn to play.

"So what's been up with you, Nelson?"

"School," replied Nelson. "These night classes are kicking my ass."

"I bet they are. Psychiatry is some deep stuff," said Connor.

"Psychology, man," said Nelson. "Why are you always getting that mixed up? How's Jade doing?"

"Fine as ever," replied Connor. "She's hanging out with Sophie and Becca today."

"Cool. Y'all getting ready for the Fourth of July barbecue?"

"Yeah," replied Connor. "Jade will finally get to meet my family. You wanna ride down with us or what?"

"I've been meaning to talk to you about that," replied Nelson. "I'm not gonna make the cookout this year."

"Why, man?" Connor asked.

"Because I haven't seen my family since Christmas, and my sister got in my ass about not visiting her and seeing my nieces."

"I understand," said Connor. "I know she was mad as hell."

"She's always mad." Nelson laughed. "I feel bad that I'm going to miss it this year though," said Nelson.

"Me too, bro. My mom's is gonna be mad at you."

"I know. That's why I'm leaving it up to you to tell her." Nelson laughed.

"Like hell you are," shouted Connor. "I'm not telling her a damn thing."

"That's cold, C."

"Sorry, man, can't do it," said Connor.

"How's work?" Nelson asked.

"Busy as ever. A lot of people trying to move before the new school year starts."

"That's a good thing," said Nelson.

"It sure is. We're looking at opening a new office in North Carolina, so I have to go to Charlotte after the holiday."

"That's what's up," said Nelson. "Is Jade going with you?"

"Nah, man, she gotta work," replied Connor. "And where the hell is Marcus?"

"Who knows?" replied Nelson. "He said he would meet us here. Something must have come up because he's always on time."

A pick-up game finally became available. Connor and Nelson won the first two games. As they were playing game three, Nelson noticed that Connor's game was off. The other team noticed it as well and used Connor's degraded capacity to their advantage.

"Man, play or warm the bench," said one of the players.

"Shut up and play," yelled Connor.

Connor and Nelson lost game three. Drenched in sweat, and huffing and puffing, Connor and Nelson sat down on the bleachers. They took off their wet T-shirts and put on dry T-shirts.

"Looking good out there, Nelson," yelled one of the girls sitting on the bleachers.

Nelson looked at the girl and smiled.

The girl smiled and said, "Who's your friend?"

"This is my man, C," replied Nelson.

"Oh," she said. "How you doin', C?"

"Hey," replied Connor. Connor raised his hand to say hello.

"Call me later, Nelson," she yelled.

Nelson smiled at the girl and waved goodbye. Connor and Nelson picked up their duffel bags and headed to the parking lot.

"I'll meet you at your place," said Connor.

* * *

Connor and Nelson relaxed and watched ESPN when they arrived at his apartment. Nelson loved sports, and ESPN was pretty much the only channel he watched.

"Yo, C, what was going on with you out there today? You were off your game, man."

"I know. I have a lot on my mind," replied Connor.

"Like what?" Nelson asked.

"Jade. Work..."

"Jade? What do you mean?"

"She doesn't want to get married," replied Connor.

"Married!" Nelson yelled. "Man, it's too soon for that!"

"Jade said the same thing." Connor chuckled.

"That's because she's smart," said Nelson, laughing.

"Every time we talk about marriage, she always says she's not ready. But man, I love Jade, and I want to spend the rest of my life with her."

"Did you tell her that?" Nelson asked.

"Of course," replied Connor. "I tell her I love her all the time."

"But what about wanting to spend the rest of your life with her. Did you tell her that?" Nelson asked more directly.

Nelson didn't want to know the answer. He knew for sure it would be yes. In the back of his mind, Nelson wanted to be the guy telling Jade that he loved her and wanted to spend the rest of his life with her. There was no getting around it, Nelson was falling for Jade. He had a clear vision as to why Connor loved her. She was special.

And to make matters worse, Nelson couldn't tell anyone how he felt about Jade.

"No. I did one better," replied Connor. "I bought an engagement ring. But now I'm thinking that I wasted a lot of money." He chuckled.

"What!" shouted Nelson. "You bought an engagement ring and didn't tell me. What's up with that?"

"Man, some things are personal," replied Connor. "I plan to ask Jade to marry me next weekend at my parents' house."

"Honestly, Connor, I think it's too soon, but if you love Jade like you say you do, I'm sure she will say yes."

"And *when* she says yes, will you be my best man?" Connor asked.

"Of course, bro. I got you," replied Nelson as he gave Connor a manly hug.

"Thanks for the chat, man. I appreciate it. I need to use your bathroom. Be right back."

"No problem, C. You want a beer?"

"Sure," replied Connor.

Connor grabbed his duffel bag and headed to the bathroom. Nelson went to the kitchen, grabbed two beers out of the fridge, and put the beers in his NY Giants can holders.

As Nelson headed back to the living room, he heard Connor yelling on the phone. Nelson assumed Connor was talking to Jade, but as he handed Connor a beer, he heard Connor say, "I told you to stop calling me."

Nelson looked at Connor and thought, *Who the hell is he talking to?*

"Damn, this girl keeps calling me," said Connor as he hung up the phone.

"Who?" Nelson asked.

"Lisa," replied Connor. "I told her time and time again to stop calling me, but she won't let up. I wish she would just leave me the hell alone."

"Is she cute?" Nelson asked playfully.

"C'mon, Nelson. I need to get this girl off my back. But yeah, man, she's cute." Connor laughed. "But seriously, man, all I did was train her, and now she won't leave me alone. I'm gonna tell my uncle to fire her crazy ass. I can't even get a cup of coffee without her following me into the break room. She calls me on my work phone for no apparent reason, and she sends me e-mails, telling me the things she wants to do in the bed, man. That girl got issues."

"Damn, C. Sounds like she wants you," said Nelson.

"Man, I gotta do something quick. She's driving me fucking crazy. Just last week, during our meeting, she rubbed my leg under the table. What kind of shit is that? I looked at her like she was crazy, and all she did was smile at me. She got the whole office thinking there's something going on between us. I avoid her at work, and let her calls go to voicemail, and she still hasn't gotten the message."

"Yo, C, you gotta nip that in the bud before it gets ugly," said Nelson.

"I know, man. I'm trying, but she ain't listening." Connor laughed. "She knows I have a girlfriend, and she won't even respect that. I'm gonna get the bitch fired."

"Man, don't get her fired," said Nelson. "That's a bit harsh. There's gotta be something else you can do."

"I can hook her up with you." Connor laughed.

"Nah, I don't need that in my life. That girl is clearly feeling you."

"So what do you suggest I do, doctor Parello?"

"Honestly, I think you should stop avoiding her. Your actions are making her want you more. She likes you, and she's acting on her emotions. I think you should play it cool. Be calm and talk to her, but here's the catch, every time you talk to her, throw something in the conversation about Jade. You know, something like, 'My girl made me lunch today,' or 'Jade likes that color too.' Sooner or later she's gonna get tired of you talking about Jade, and she will leave you alone all together."

"Damn, Nelson, that's some good shit right there," shouted Connor. "You're gonna make a damn good psychiatrist one day."

"Psychologist, man, psychologist," said Nelson. "There's a difference."

"Whatever, bro. Thanks for the help. Send me a bill," said Connor as he finished his beer.

"Don't worry, I will," said Nelson.

Connor laughed as he walked out the door. As he drove home, he thought about Nelson's suggestions and figured he would put Nelson's remedy to work. He tapped the phone icon on his Bluetooth and called Lisa.

"Hey, Lisa, it's Connor."

"I know. What's up?"

"I just want to apologize for the way I spoke to you earlier. I'm sorry about that. We work together, so we gotta talk, but I would appreciate it if you only called me at work for work related issues. Also, you need to respect my relationship with Jade and not call or text me on my cell."

"Okay, Connor," said Lisa. "No problem."

The house was quiet when Connor got home. Connor dropped his duffel bag near the door, turned off the lights, and went to the bedroom to check on Jade. Then he took a quick shower and got in bed. But Connor couldn't sleep. He was overwhelmed with excitement and joy for his upcoming surprise. Connor crawled out of the bed and went to his office.

He unlocked his desk drawer and pulled out Jade's engagement ring. It was an elegant diamond ring. Platinum, of course. Nothing but the best for his girl. And even though the ring would set Connor back almost three thousand dollars, to him it didn't matter. Money wasn't an object when it came to Jade.

Connor locked the ring back in the drawer and went back to bed. He looked at Jade as she slept, and felt blessed to have met such a wonderful girl. Connor leaned over and kissed Jade on the top of her head. "Good night, love," he whispered.

10

Jade and Connor were in high spirits and ready to celebrate the Fourth of July holiday away from home.

On Thursday she and Connor cleaned the house and started to pack. When Connor was done packing, he sat on the bed and watched Jade finish packing her things.

"Ooh baby, those panties are sexy," said Connor. "Are they new?"

"They sure are," replied Jade. "I got them for you."

"I sure hope I get to see them on you."

"You might," said Jade. "Well, I'm all done. Just gotta throw my toiletries in my bag in the morning."

"Don't forget your bathing suit," said Connor.

"Oh yeah, thanks for reminding me." Jade grabbed her bathing suit out of the drawer and threw it in her suitcase.

"Now get your butt in the bed," joked Connor. "We gotta get up early and hit the road."

"Connor, can I talk to you about something?" Jade asked as she sat down on the bed.

"Baby, you can talk to me about anything," replied Connor. "What's up?"

Jade didn't know where to begin. She didn't want to argue or upset Connor, but she had to ask him about Lisa.

"Well, what is it?"

"I keep thinking about that Lisa girl, and I—"

"What!" Connor shouted. "Why are you thinking about her? Hold up. Let me mute the TV."

Connor sat up and pressed the mute button on the remote control. He threw the remote on the bed and looked at Jade.

"Jade, we just work together, that's it," he continued.

"Calm down, Connor. I don't want to argue. But I feel we need to talk about this because it's bothering me."

"I'm calm. I just don't know why you're letting her get to you," said Connor.

"Does she still call you?"

"Only at work," replied Connor. "Jade, Lisa and I work together, so we have to talk, but I told Lisa that she needed to respect my relationship with you and not call or text me on my cell. You are *it* for me, Jade. There is no one else, and there will never be anyone else."

"So then, you took care of it?" Jade asked.

"Absolutely," replied Connor.

Connor did take care of it. He just hoped Lisa would stick to her agreement and not call or text him anymore.

* * *

Early Friday morning, Jade and Connor had a quick breakfast at home, cleaned the kitchen, jumped in Connor's BMW, and headed to Georgia for the Ellis family's Fourth of July barbecue.

Jade was so excited. This trip would mark her first mini vacay since graduation, and she was ready to enjoy herself. She couldn't wait to get out of Virginia for the long weekend.

"Let's put the top down and cruise," said Jade.

"I was thinking the same thing," said Connor.

Jade and Connor prayed for safe travels and headed south to Georgia.

The Ellis family's Fourth of July barbecue was an annual cook-out hosted by Connor's parents. Family and friends from near and far attended as well as a few EHS employees that felt more comfortable hanging out with Connor's family than their own. The event was just shy of a family reunion, even though it seemed like one to Connor. Most of the guests were Connor's family members that lived in the States, but a few of his relatives that lived in Italy made the yearly trip.

Jade was a bit nervous as this was her first Ellis family barbecue, however, she was looking forward to meeting Connor's family and seeing where he grew up. Although knowing Mr. and Mrs. Ellis put Jade at ease, she still wanted to make a good impression for the rest of Connor's family.

Connor turned on the radio and held Jade's hand as they cruised down the highway. From time to time, he would pull Jade's hand up to his mouth and kiss the back of her hand. Jade loved it when Connor did that. His lips were soft, and his kisses felt good.

About six hours into the drive, Connor pulled into the parking lot of Dell's Diner.

"You hungry?"

"A little bit," replied Jade.

"I'm starving." Connor laughed. "This diner looks pretty decent. Let's go check out the menu."

"Baby, every diner has the same food," said Jade. "Pancakes, burgers, fries, and club sandwiches." Jade laughed.

"A nice thick burger sounds good to me," said Connor.

Connor opened the door and followed Jade inside the diner. They immediately smelled the aroma of bacon, pancakes, and hot coffee.

"Welcome to Dell's," yelled a short lady from behind the counter. Her voice was loud and perky, and it got Jade's attention. Jade looked at the short lady and smiled.

Jade and Connor walked past the "seat yourself" sign and toward a booth near the window.

"Someone will be with y'all in a minute," said the short lady.

"Thank you," said Connor as he and Jade sat down.

"The seats are comfortable," said Connor.

Connor grabbed two menus from the menu holder. He handed one to Jade but Jade was preoccupied with her phone.

"Everything okay?" Connor asked.

"Yeah. I missed my mom's call," replied Jade.

"She'll call you back," said Connor.

"I'm gonna call her," said Jade.

Jade called her mother and talked to her while she looked at the menu. She told her mother that she would feel better if her family was going to be at the cookout. Jade's mother assured her that Connor would make sure she was comfortable and that she enjoyed herself.

"How y'all doing? My name is Emily, and I'll be taking care of y'all. What can I get y'all to drink?"

"I'll have a sweet tea," replied Jade.

"Make that two please," replied Connor.

"Okay. Be right back."

Five minutes later, Emily returned with two red Coca-Cola cups. She placed the cups on the table and smiled at Connor.

"So have we decided yet?" Emily asked.

"Yes," replied Connor. "Baby, what do you want?"

"Aww, that's sweet," said Emily. "Letting the lady order first. Your mother raised you right, young man." Emily smiled at Jade and asked, "What can I get you, sweetie?"

"I'll have the chicken club sandwich," replied Jade. "No cheese please."

"Good choice. That's my fav-fav, but with cheese, of course," said Emily as she smacked her hips and laughed. "And for you, young man? What can I get you?"

"I'll have the bacon cheeseburger," replied Connor. "Well done, please."

"Fries come with both, is that okay?" Emily asked.

"Sure," replied Connor.

"Great! Be right back," said Emily.

Twenty minutes later, Emily returned to the table. She placed the chicken club in front of Jade and the bacon cheeseburger in front of Connor. "Y'all enjoy, okay," she said. "I'll be back to check on y'all in a few."

"Thanks, Emily," said Jade.

* * *

A few hours later, Connor and Jade arrived at his parents' house. The sun was setting, filling the sky with beautiful shades of blue and orange.

The Ellis house was huge. Jade wondered why two people would want to live in such a big house. It didn't make sense to her.

"Your parents like staying in this big house alone?" Jade asked.

"They sure do," replied Connor. "But they're not alone, they have each other. One day it'll be ours, and we can fill it up with lots of kids."

"I would love to live in that house," said Jade.

Connor got out of the car and hurried to the passenger side to help Jade. Jade smiled as she waved to Mr. and Mrs. Ellis. Mrs. Ellis waved back, and Mr. Ellis nodded his head in response. Connor took their luggage out of the trunk and headed toward the house.

"Hey, Mom and Dad," said Connor. "How y'all doing?"

"Great, son, simply great," his father replied. "How are you doing?"

"Tired." Connor laughed.

"Come here and give me some sugar," said his mother. "I missed you, baby."

"I missed you too," said Connor.

Connor shook his father's hand and gave his mother a hug and a kiss. His mother looked over his shoulder and asked, "And where is my other son?"

"Nelson went to Florida to see his family," replied Connor.

"Oh, that's nice," said his mother. "Look at you, Jade. Just as beautiful as ever. How are you doing, sweetheart?"

"I'm doing great," replied Jade. "How are you and Mr. Ellis doing?"

"We're doing fine," replied Mr. Ellis.

"It's nice to see y'all again," said Jade. "And thank you for your hospitality. I really appreciate it."

"Oh, don't you worry about any of that," said Julia. "We have plenty of room. Connor will show you where everything is and take you upstairs. I know you're tired, so I'll see you in the morning."

"Thank you," said Jade.

When Jade stepped into the house, she was met with music and laughter. Everyone was having a good time. People were all over the house. Some were dancing and a few people were eating, and others were playing cards. Little kids were running from one end of the house to the other end of the house.

Jade smelled the scent of peach cobbler and desperately wanted some, but she decided against it. All she wanted to do was go upstairs and go to sleep.

"All these people," said Jade. "You *do* have a big family."

"Wait until tomorrow," said Connor. "More of the Ellis tribe are coming, so get ready."

"Thanks for the heads up," said Jade jokingly.

"C'mon. Let me take you upstairs."

Jade grabbed her luggage and followed Connor upstairs to his bedroom. She put her suitcase on the bed and started to unpack.

"Baby, what are you doing?" Connor asked. "Don't you wanna meet my family?"

"Connor, I'm tired," whined Jade. "Can it wait until tomorrow?"

"Tell you what," said Connor. "Let's just go downstairs for a few minutes, that's all, okay."

"You promise?"

"I promise," replied Connor.

Jade and Connor held hands as they went downstairs. When they reached the foyer, his cousin Natalia was standing near the large floor vase looking for her son.

"Hey, cuz, what's up?" Natalia asked.

"Not much," replied Connor as he gave Natalia a hug and a kiss. "This is Jade. Jade, this is one of my favorite cousins, Natalia."

"Hi, Jade. It's nice to meet you. Love the hair," said Natalia.

"Thank you," said Jade. "Nice to meet you too."

"Excuse me," said Natalia. "I gotta go find little Avery before he breaks something."

"Yeah, you better." Connor laughed.

As Natalia walked away, she said, "Hopefully we'll get to hang out this weekend, Jade."

"Sure," said Jade.

Jade followed Connor into the huge family room. Everyone was chatting and enjoying themselves, as music played in the background.

"Hey family," yelled Connor with a big smile on his face.

"Yo, Conario, what up," someone yelled. "Good to see you, man. Sorry I missed your graduation," he continued as he held up his bottle of beer.

"My man," yelled someone else. "How the hell are you, bro?"

"Yo, cuz, you gained weight," said someone else. "I guess that cutie is feeding you well."

"Connor, Connor," said a little girl as she ran to him and wrapped her small arms around his waist.

Jade looked down and saw the cutest little girl looking up a Connor.

"Hey, Mariah. What's up, little mama?"

"Nuttin," replied Mariah. "Is she your girlfriend?"

"Yes, Mariah, and her name is Jade," replied Connor.

"Connor got a girlfriend, Connor got a girlfriend," yelled Mariah as she ran back to play with her cousins.

"That girl is something else." Connor laughed.

"She's adorable," said Jade.

Connor saw his uncle and cousins standing near the grand piano. He grabbed Jade's hand and took her to meet his family.

"Family, this is Jade. Jade, these are my cousins, and that's my uncle."

"Hello," said Jade.

"Hi, young lady," said a tall, dark-skinned, baldheaded guy. "I'm Sean. This here is Avery, and that's our uncle, Mateo."

"It's nice to meet y'all," said Jade.

"Same here," they replied.

"Yo, cuz. Take Jade in the back to meet the ladies and then come back so we can catch up," said Sean.

"Okay, cuz. Be right back."

Connor looked at Jade and remembered his promise.

"Baby, go upstairs and get some sleep," he said. "I'm gonna hang out with my cousins for a little while."

"Okay," said Jade. "I guess you'll have to miss your massage."

"What!" yelled Connor. "Damn, that sounds so good. Can I get a raincheck?"

"Nope." Jade laughed.

Jade kissed Connor and headed upstairs. She admired the decor and the shades of blue and beige that surrounded his room. Connor's bed was huge, and Jade was ready to get in it.

Jade unpacked a few of her things. She hung her new summer dress in the closet. With her sexy nightie in hand, she grabbed her toiletry bag, headed to the bathroom, and took a shower.

The soap lathered up more than she had ever seen soap lather up before, and the aroma of the soap was exhilarating. Jade fell in love with the soap and wanted some of her own.

After Jade showered, she crawled into Connor's bed and sent her mother a text: *We're in GA. Gnite. Luv U.* Then Jade turned off the lights and went to sleep.

11

Jade was awakened by the commotion outside. She rubbed the sleep out of her eyes and looked over at Connor's side of the bed. He wasn't there, and he hadn't slept in his bed. Jade glanced toward the door and noticed that Connor's luggage hadn't been moved. She looked at the time on her phone. It was almost ten o'clock. Where was Connor?

Jade peeped out the window and saw the huge in-ground pool. Lots of tables and chairs outlined the pool. White tablecloths covered the tables and decorative centerpieces sat in the middle of each table. A few guys were putting up a jungle gym and a small water slide. Jade noticed that the dance floor was already laid down, and the DJ was almost done setting up his equipment.

Jade got excited. She took a shower and got dressed. On her way downstairs, she smelled bacon, eggs, and fresh coffee brewing. The food smelled delicious, but all Jade wanted was a hot cup of coffee.

"Good morning," said Jade as she walked into the kitchen.

"Good morning," said Julia. "That is a lovely dress."

"Thank you," said Jade.

"How did you sleep?"

"Pretty good," replied Jade. "Have you seen Connor?"

"Not yet, sweetie," replied Julia. "He stayed up late talking and drinking with his cousins. Help yourself to whatever you want. Do you drink coffee?"

"Yes, ma'am," replied Jade.

"Good. Well, there's coffee and cappuccino right over there in the coffee nook."

"Thank you, Mrs. Ellis. By the way, that soap in Connor's bathroom, where can I find it?"

"Oh, you like it?" Julia asked.

"Yes, ma'am," replied Jade.

"We get it shipped here from Italy," said Julia. "It's part of our home care package that we send to our new homeowners. Remind me to give you a few bars before you leave."

"I sure will," said Jade. "Thank you."

"My pleasure," said Julia. "Connor tells me your parents are in the hair care business."

"Yes, ma'am. They own a few hair care stores in Virginia," said Jade.

"That sounds exciting," said Julia.

"It was when I was younger," said Jade. "My brother and I worked in the store when we were in high school. We had a lot of fun."

"I'm sure y'all did."

Jade smiled at Mrs. Ellis. She then poured herself a cup of coffee and joined Natalia at the table.

"Good morning, Natalia."

"Hey, Jade," said Natalia. "Sit down and keep me company. This boy does not want to eat today."

"I don't want it, Mommy," whined the handsome little boy.

"Avery, se non mangi. Non potrai uscire a giocare. Quindi, cosa sara?"

Avery quickly picked up his fork, stabbed a piece of the pancake, and put it in his mouth.

"What did you say to him?" Jade asked.

"That he wouldn't be able to go outside and play if he doesn't eat."

"Wow, I'm impressed," said Jade. "The only thing Connor says to me in Italian is '*Ti amo*, Giada and bella.' And he says it *so* sexy."

"I bet." Natalia laughed. "How long have y'all been dating?"

"Almost a year," replied Jade.

"Oh, cool. I can tell Connor really likes you. He hasn't brought anyone home in a long time. Don't tell him I said that." Natalia laughed.

"My lips are sealed," said Jade. "Your son is adorable."

"Thank you," replied Natalia. "He's my little crumb-snatcher."

"How old is he?"

"Four, and a terror," replied Natalia.

"I'm not a terror, Mom, I'm a boy."

"Yes, you are." Natalia laughed. "Now eat your food so I can get you dressed."

Avery ate his pancakes. When he was done, he picked up his sippy cup and took a long swallow.

"Ah," he sighed.

Avery put the cup down on the table and wiped his mouth with the back of his hand.

"All done, Mommy," he said.

"Good job, Avery. Now let's get you dressed. I'll see you later, Jade."

"Okay, Natalia."

Jade was getting hungry. She walked over to the island and looked at the food display. She picked up a plate and put a few pieces of bacon on it and a spoonful of fruit salad. Jade was impressed with the extravagant spread and she wondered what the barbecue spread was going to look like.

"You cooked all this food yourself, Mrs. Ellis?"

"No way, baby. My sisters and in-laws helped me. They usually get the cooking started, then I come in and finish up. And in about ten minutes when I close this kitchen, the youngsters that stayed up all night will come in and eat and then clean up the kitchen."

"Ah, here comes my baby now," said Julia as Connor walked into the kitchen.

"Hey, Ma," said Connor as he gave his mother a hug.

"We were looking for you," said his mother as she winked at Jade.

"Sorry, ladies. I fell asleep downstairs with Sean and them," said Connor. "Did you sleep well, Jade?"

"Like a baby," she replied.

"You must have because you look gorgeous," said Connor. "I would give you a kiss, but I haven't brushed my teeth yet."

"Ew, yuck." Jade laughed.

Connor made himself a cup of coffee and sat down next to Jade. Julia took off her apron and hung it on the pantry door.

"I'll see y'all later," said Julia.

"Okay, Mom. See you later."

"Your mom is so sweet," said Jade.

"She loves having her family around," said Connor.

"I can tell," said Jade. "When are you going to get showered and dressed?"

"Don't know. I was just gonna keep this on," replied Connor.

"That's gross, Connor. You had those clothes on since yesterday morning."

Connor laughed and said, "I'm joking, Jade. I'm gonna take a shower in a few minutes. Why?"

"My period came, and I need to get some tampons."

"Damn, so I won't be able to see those sexy panties this weekend."

"Guess not." Jade laughed.

"That's messed up," said Connor. "Let me go shower and take you to the store. You might as well come upstairs with me. The ladies are about to swarm this kitchen, and believe me, they will put you to work if they see you in here."

"I'm right behind you," said Jade.

Jade followed Connor upstairs. While Connor showered, Jade sat in a soft blue chair near the window and attempted to read her book. She looked out the window and saw Mr. Ellis cooking on the grill. Connor's uncle was on another grill, and a hefty guy was standing in front of a large pit, grilling all kinds of meat. *We're in for a real treat*, thought Jade. The smell of the charcoal and barbecue filled the air and seeped into the house.

Jade decided to wait for Connor outside. She put her book down on the nightstand, grabbed her shades and went downstairs.

As Jade stepped onto the deck, she acknowledged Connor's family and made her way to the picnic tables. She found an empty table and sat down. She did a quick 360 around the yard and was astounded by the beautiful piece of property that surrounded her.

"So you must be Jade," said a man from behind her. Jade turned around and saw a tall man standing behind her.

"Yes, I am," she said.

"Nice to meet you. I'm Antonio."

"Nice to meet you too," said Jade.

"So are you enjoying yourself?"

"I am," replied Jade.

"We do this every year," said Antonio.

"I know. Connor told me." Jade laughed. "This whole setup must take a lot of time and work."

"Yeah, but the whole family helps, so it's not bad. Do you want something to drink?"

"No thanks," replied Jade.

"Well Connor was right, sei davvero bella."

"Thank you, Antonio."

"You speak Italian?" Antonio asked, surprised.

"Not at all." Jade laughed. "But I know bella. Connor says a few things to me in Italian, and then I look them up on the internet."

"Cool. Speak of the devil. Here comes my cousin now, looking all dapper and shit."

Jade turned around, and sure enough, Connor looked handsome as ever.

"You ready to go baby?" Connor asked.

"Yes," replied Jade.

"Where y'all going cuz?"

"Stop being so damn nosey," said Connor. "We'll be right back."

"Okay. See y'all later," said Antonio.

Connor drove Jade to the closest convenient store. He wanted to hurry back so he could eat and dance with her.

As Connor drove, he thought about his surprise for Jade. He had told his cousins about his plan last night, and they all wanted to see the ring, so Connor went upstairs, snuck into his room while Jade slept, and got the ring out of his suitcase.

"What's with the Kool-Aid smile?" Jade asked.

"Girl, what are you talking about?"

"Connor, you're smiling from ear to ear."

"I'm just happy you're here with me and my family."

Connor parked in front of Walgreens. Jade jumped out of the car and ran inside the store. She picked up a small box of tampons, paid for her item, and ran out of the store.

"Okay, let's go," said Jade as she got in the car.

"Cool. When we get back, I wanna dance with you," said Connor.

"Of course," said Jade.

When Jade and Connor returned to the house, Jade ran upstairs to the bathroom. She washed up, put on perfume, and hurried back downstairs.

Jade found Connor sitting at a table with Antonio, Sean, and Avery. Antonio and Sean were drinking beers and chatting. Avery was smoking a Black and Mild and talking to Connor.

"Hey, baby," said Connor.

"Hey," said Jade. "Did you eat yet?"

"Sure did," replied Connor.

"Oh, okay," said Jade. "I'm gonna go make me a plate and find Natalia."

"Okay, but you probably won't find her with all these people here," said Connor.

Jade looked around the backyard. It was filled with kids and adults enjoying themselves.

"How long does everyone usually stay?"

"All night long," replied Sean.

"Go make yourself a plate and come back over here with us," said Connor.

"Okay. I'll be right back," said Jade.

When Jade stepped away from the table, Connor got to work assembling his plan.

"Okay fellas," said Connor. "Y'all remember what we discussed last night?"

"We got you cuz," replied Sean.

"Cool. So while y'all are distracting Jade, I'm gonna go inside and get her parents. So keep her occupied, a'ight."

"We're on it," said Avery.

Connor's cousins followed Jade to the grill area while he ran inside the house to get her parents.

"Excuse me," said Connor as he walked into the sunroom. "Mr. and Mrs. Simpson, it's a pleasure to see you again. My cousins are keeping Jade occupied while I sneak y'all outside. Y'all ready to surprise Jade?"

"Absolutely," replied Tanya.

Jade's parents followed Connor outside to the table he had prepared for them. His parents followed closely behind.

"Can I get you or your wife anything, Mr. Simpson?" Connor asked.

"No, son, we're fine," replied Mr. Simpson.

"Okay, good," said Connor. "I'm going to get Jade. Be right back."

Connor smiled and went to get Jade. He knew Jade wanted her parents to be there and that she would be overjoyed when she saw them.

Connor had put his plan together after his man to man talk with Jade's father. During their conversation, Jade's father wanted to know Connor's intentions. Connor candidly told him that he loved Jade and that he wanted to spend the rest of his life with her. Jade's father didn't have any objections to Connor asking Jade for her hand in marriage, so Connor quickly put his plan into action.

Connor called his parents and told them that he was going to ask Jade to marry him during the Fourth of July cookout. His parents were excited and eager to help him with his grand plan.

"You know, son, the fireworks sound off at nine," his father said. "I think it would be awesome if you asked Jade right before then, so when she says yes, the fireworks will seal the deal."

Connor agreed with his father. All he needed now was a place for Jade's parents to stay for the weekend.

When Connor told his parents that he didn't want the Simpsons to stay in a hotel, his mother butted in, "Say no more, baby, we got it covered."

Connor felt assured knowing that his parents had his back. He was grateful for his parents and their unselfishness in helping him make the day special for Jade.

"Well, I see my cousins are holding you hostage," said Connor.

"Not at all," said Jade. "They've been keeping me company."

"Thanks guys. I got it from here," said Connor.

"See y'all later," said Jade as she waved goodbye.

"I hope your food is still hot," said Connor.

"It's warm," said Jade. "I nibbled while your cousins entertained me."

"Cool," said Connor. "I hope our table is still empty."

"Stop worrying," said Jade. "I thought we were supposed to relax and have a good time this weekend."

"You know what, you're right," said Connor.

"So then why are you worrying about a table? If the table is full, we can sit somewhere else."

"True," said Connor.

Connor grabbed Jade's plate and hand and led her through the crowd. As they approached the table, Jade peeped through the crowd and saw a few heads at their table.

"Baby, it looks like we gotta find another table." Jade laughed.

"Maybe. Let's at least go check and see if there are any empty seats left," said Connor.

"Okay," said Jade.

As they got closer to the table, Jade saw a familiar face. She took a double look and realized she was staring at her mother. Jade stopped dead in her tracks, released her hand from Connor's grip, and covered her mouth in surprise. Jade's emotions got the best of her and she started to cry.

"Jade, I wanted to surprise you, so I arranged to have your parents join us this weekend."

"But how did you…"

"Don't worry about that," said Connor.

"Thank you, Connor. I love you so much," said Jade.

Jade gave her parents a kiss and sat down next to her mother. Connor sat down and gave his parents a thank you nod for helping him pull off the surprise successfully.

"What are y'all doing here?" Jade asked. "When did you get here? Where are y'all staying?"

"Relax, sweetie," said her mother. "Connor invited us, and since we had nothing else to do, we decided to take him up on his offer. It was very thoughtful of Connor to invite us."

"Yes it was," agreed Jade's father.

"Are Justin and Zaria here?" Jade asked.

"No, baby," replied her mother. "They had other plans."

"I can't believe y'all are here," shouted Jade. "This is so awesome!"

Jade was beyond happy and too excited to finish eating. Connor stood up and grabbed Jade's hand, and they joined his cousins on the dance floor.

"Okay, family," yelled the DJ. "This next jam is for the grown-ups. Sorry, little kiddies, it's time for y'all to take a break."

LUV by Tory Lanez filled the air. Jade looked into Connor's eyes, amazed at what he did for her. Jade thanked Connor with a passionate tongue kiss.

"Hey, cuz, cut that mess out," said Antonio.

Connor laughed and said, "Don't hate, playa. You just stay over there and mind your business."

Jade and Antonio's date laughed out loud.

Then the DJ played "I'll Make Love to You" by Boyz II Men. Connor squeezed Jade around her waist and pulled her closer to him. And as Connor held her tight, he whispered the sultry lyrics in her ear.

"Okay, family," yelled the DJ. "This next jam is for everyone." As the beat to the "Wobble" started, the kids screamed and ran onto the dance floor.

After Connor and Jade danced, they headed over to the fire pit, where Connor introduced Jade to more of his family.

"Hey, TJ, where you been all day?" Connor asked.

"Work," replied TJ. "Who's your friend?"

"Everyone, this is Jade," said Connor.

"Jade, that's TJ and his wife, Vicky. That's Wilson and his girl-friend, April. And that's Julio and his wife, Deidre."

Jade waved her hand and said hello to Connor's family.

"Hey, Jade. Come sit down over here," said Vicky. "You want something to drink? Baby, get Jade a daiquiri out of the cooler."

"Thank you. I love daiquiris," said Jade.

"Me too," said Vicky. "So where are you from?"

"Virginia," replied Jade.

"How are the beaches there?" April asked.

"They're pretty nice," replied Jade.

"Well, what I want to know, is do you have a job?" Deidre asked.

"Yes, ma'am. I work for a marketing firm," replied Jade.

"Cuz, you darn found yourself a cute girl with a job," said Deidre. "You did good, Connor."

Everyone laughed at Deidre's comment.

Jade sipped on her daiquiri and chatted with the ladies. Connor drank a beer and chatted with the fellas.

"Excuse me, ladies. I'll be right back," said Jade.

"Okay, hurry back," said Vicky.

Jade went inside the house to use the bathroom. Before she headed back downstairs, she touched up her makeup, sprayed per-fume on her dress, and checked her cell phone.

When Jade returned to the fire pit, Connor wasn't there. Jade sat quietly and listened to the ladies discuss their cruise plans.

"We're all set for the cruise, ladies," said Vicky.

"Good, 'cause I'm ready to go," shouted April.

Deidre looked at April and said, "Don't pack all that shit you packed last year, April."

"I won't." April laughed.

As the day turned to night, the outdoor lights lit up the backyard. Jade adored the way the pool lights colored the water in shades of blue and green. A few of the older kids were still playing in the pool. The little kids were running around, and the toddlers were wrapped up in blankets sitting on their mama's laps.

Jade discreetly searched the backyard for Connor, but he wasn't anywhere in sight. A few minutes later, Connor walked up behind Jade and put his hands on her shoulders, startling her.

"You scared me, Connor." Jade laughed.

"Sorry, babe. My bad. The fireworks are starting soon, and I want to get a good spot."

"Fireworks too? Wow, your family really knows how to throw a good barbecue."

"That's how we do," said Vicky.

"It was a pleasure meeting y'all," said Jade.

"Same here," said the ladies.

Connor was getting anxious. It was almost time for his grand finale, and he couldn't wait to see the look on Jade's face. Connor and Jade were halfway across the dance floor when her favorite song came on.

"Did you do this too?" Jade asked.

"Nope," Connor replied. "Let's dance."

"What about our good spot for the fireworks?"

"This entire yard is a good spot," replied Connor.

Connor kissed Jade as he danced with her. As the song was ending, Connor grabbed Jade's hand and led her to the DJ table. Connor grabbed the mic, cleared his throat, and began to speak.

"Excuse me," said Connor. "Can I have your attention please?"

Connor's family stopped what they were doing and gave him their undivided attention.

"Mom, Dad, can y'all come up here with Jade's parents please?"

As their parents made their way to the DJ table, Connor continued his speech. "I just want to thank my parents for hosting another amazing Fourth of July barbecue. And to our family and friends, thank y'all for joining us. Having you all here with us brings joy to my parents' heart. It means a lot to us that y'all continue to show up year after year. We really appreciate it.

"For those of you that have not met my girlfriend yet, here she is. Her name is Jade, and if y'all would allow me two minutes of your time, I would like to ask her a question."

Connor looked at Jade and noticed the puzzled look on her face. But Connor didn't let that bother him, he continued with his surprise.

"Connor, what are you doing?" Jade whispered.

Connor stepped closer to Jade, looked into her eyes, and said,

"Jade, from the moment I saw you, I loved you. Everything inside me told me that you were the one for me. I think about you from the moment I wake up until the moment I close my eyes."

Connor took a deep breath and continued, "Jade, you have brought so much joy and happiness into my life, and I thank God that our paths crossed. I'm ready to spend the rest of my life with you."

As Connor got down on one knee, Jade gasped and covered her mouth with her hands. He pulled a small black velvet box out of his pocket and opened it.

"Jade Marie Simpson," said Connor. "Will you do me the honor of being my wife?"

"Yes, Connor, yes," cried Jade.

Tears rolled down Jade's face. Connor stood up and placed the ring on Jade's finger. As Connor's family clapped their hands and shouted congratulatory cheers, he kissed Jade and hugged her tight.

"Ti amo, Giada, ti amo," Connor whispered.

"I love you too," said Jade.

A few seconds later, the thunderous sounds of fireworks filled the air as the sky was illuminated with bright colors. *Right on time*, thought Connor.

"I'm so glad you guys were here to see this," cried Jade as she hugged her parents.

"It was all part of the plan," said her father as he shook Connor's hand.

Connor's mother grabbed Jade's hands and said, "If I had to choose a daughter, I would choose you, Jade. Thank you for making my son happy."

"Aww. Thank you, Mrs. Ellis. Connor makes me happy too."

Jade looked at the ring on her finger. It was exquisite.

12

Connor was packed and all set for his trip to Charlotte. It was his first business trip, and he was excited. Connor stood near the door, waiting to say goodbye to Jade.

"Hey, Jade. I'm about to hit the road," he yelled. "Where are you?"

"I'm on the toilet," yelled Jade. "Be right there."

"Dang, girl. You've been peeing a lot lately."

"That's what water does to the body," said Jade.

Jade flushed the toilet and ran to the front door.

"Why are you leaving so early?" Jade asked. "I thought we would at least have breakfast together."

"Sorry, baby," said Connor. "I have a five-hour drive ahead of me, and I want to beat the traffic. I'll see you Wednesday evening, okay."

"Okay, baby. Drive safe. Call me when you get all checked in."

Connor kissed Jade goodbye and walked out the door. Jade locked the door behind him and jumped back in the bed. She turned on the television to TCM. *Casablanca* was coming on. "Great," she said. Jade loved the old black and white movies. The actors were handsome, and the actresses were beautiful.

Humphrey Bogart was her favorite. To Jade, Bogie was myste-
riously handsome, and any movie he starred in was on the top of her
watch list. After *Casablanca*, she watched *Bogie in the Big Sleep*.

After her movie time, she washed clothes. While the clothes
were in the wash, Jade boiled two eggs and made a fruit smoothie
with pineapple juice, yogurt, and honey.

When the eggs were done, Jade put them in a small bowl,
grabbed her smoothie and went into the family room to watch
another movie. As Jade was deshelling the eggs, her phone rang.

Who the heck is FaceTiming me this early?

"Hey, Jade," yelled Becca.

"Hey, Becca, what's up, girl?"

"Nothing much," replied Becca. "I'm on my way to the gym.
Wanna join me?"

"Thanks for the invite, but I'm staying in today. Why are you
going so early?"

"Because it's supposed to storm later, and I don't want to get
caught in all that mess," replied Becca.

"I know what you mean."

"Okay then. I'll talk to you later," said Becca. "Oh, wait. Did
you get my text about Ava Scott?"

"I sure did, and thanks, Becca. I really appreciate it."

"Ava does great work," said Becca. "She did my cousin's wedding
last year, and it was absolutely gorgeous. I know you and Connor will
like her. Talk to you later, girl. I gotta go."

Becca blew Jade a virtual kiss and disconnected the call.

Jade ate her eggs and drank her smoothie as she watched television. Soon after she ate, she felt herself getting tired. Her eyes slowly
closed, opened, and closed again. A few hours later, Jade received a
call from Connor.

"Hey, baby. How are you?"

"Good," replied Jade.

"I just wanted to hear your voice," said Connor. "You sound so
tired. You okay?"

"Yeah, I'm good," replied Jade. "Are you in Charlotte already?"

"Nope. I should be there in about an hour or so," replied Connor. "What have you been doing besides sleeping?" Connor laughed.

"Washing clothes," replied Jade. "And you left your underwear on the floor again."

"My bad," said Connor. "I miss you already."

"I miss you too. How many of these trips are you going to have to take?"

"I have no idea," replied Connor. "Hopefully not a lot. When I get back, I'm gonna make love to you *all night long*."

"Ooh, that sounds good, but I don't know if I can wait that long. I want you now."

"Girl, don't make me turn this car around," joked Connor. "Call you when I get there, sweetie. Love you."

"I love you too," said Jade.

After Jade put the clothes in the dryer, she vacuumed the family room and the living room. Then she cleaned the bathrooms. When Jade was done with the bathrooms, she polished the furniture and cleaned up Connor's office. Jade wanted Connor's office to be clean and tidy when he returned home.

After Jade cleaned up, she took a shower. Then she put on a pair of sweat shorts and a tank top and climbed in bed to relax and enjoy the rest of her day.

When Jade's phone rang again, she smiled thinking it was Connor, but it wasn't. It was a call from a number she didn't recognize.

"Hello," said Jade cautiously.

"Hey, Jade, how are you?"

"Nelson?"

"Yeah. It's me."

"Hey, Nelson, what's up?"

"Not much. I just called Connor, but he didn't answer."

"He's on the road."

"Oh yeah, that's right, I completely forgot. Well, how are you doing anyway?" Nelson asked again.

"Good," replied Jade.

"I asked you that already, didn't I?" Nelson laughed.

"Yeah." Jade laughed.

"Well, I'll try Connor again later, and if you get bored and want some company, just let me know, okay."

"Okay, I'll keep that in mind," said Jade.

Jade hung up. "Want some company," she said to herself. "Why would I call him for that?" Jade figured Nelson had a few beers and was feeling mellow. Before Jade was able to get comfortable, her phone rang again. She looked at her phone and smiled.

"Hey, boo," she said.

"Hey, baby, I'm all checked in."

"Oh, good. I'm glad you made it safely."

"Me too," said Connor. "It was a smooth ride. Now you sound wide awake." Connor laughed.

"I am," said Jade. "How's the hotel?"

"Nice. I just wish you were here to keep me company," replied Connor.

"Aww, me too, baby," said Jade. "So August is coming."

"Yes, it is. And what's so special about August?"

"Connor," whined Jade.

Connor laughed and said, "I know. It's your birthday. I already got that covered. Jade?"

"Yes."

"When I get home, I want to talk to you about a wedding date, okay."

"Okay," said Jade. "Oh, your boy called me looking for you. Apparently, he forgot about your trip."

"Thanks. I'll call him tomorrow," said Connor.

"Okie-dokie," said Jade.

"My uncle and I are going to get something to eat, so I'll talk to you later."

"Okay. Love you," said Jade.

"Love you more," said Connor.

By early evening, the rain clouds were rolling in. Jade decided to run out and get dinner before the rain came. Vinny's sounded good, but Jade was not in the mood to see Renz.

After Jade folded the laundry and put the clothes away, she called Vinny's and placed an order. Then Jade changed into a pair of jeans, covered her tank top with a cardigan sweater, and put on her Nike's. She grabbed her pouch and keys and headed out the door.

There weren't any available parking spots in front of Vinny's when Jade arrived. She decided to park in the rear parking lot instead of waiting for a spot out front. When Jade stepped inside the restaurant, she noticed that Vinny was back, which meant that Renz was gone. *Good*, she thought.

"Hey, Vinny, welcome back," yelled Jade.

"Thanks, Jade. How have you been?" Vinny asked.

"Great!" Jade replied. "Look what happened while you were away."

Jade extended her hand to show Vinny her engagement ring.

"Oh my, that is gorgeous," said Vinny. "Congratulations!"

"Thank you," said Jade. "Now how was your vacation?"

"Lovely," replied Vinny. "The kids enjoyed Disney, but they drove the wifey nuts. What can I get you, dear?"

"Oh, my bad. I called in my usual," said Jade.

"One shrimp scampi coming right up," said Vinny.

"Thanks, Vinny."

Jade sat down and waited for her food. She heard the loud thunder and looked out the window. It was getting dark out. Becca was right. It was going to storm.

"Your order is ready, Jade," said Vinny.

Jade hurried to the counter and paid for her food.

"Thanks, Vinny," she said quickly. "Gotta go."

"Drive safe, dear."

"Okay, thanks," said Jade as she ran out the door.

Jade jumped in the car and headed home. The rain got heavier and heavier as she got closer to home. Jade could barely see the cars in front of her. She slowed down and put the wipers on full speed.

When Jade got home, she parked her car and ran upstairs. As she entered the apartment, she hit the light switch near the front door and was thankful that she didn't lose power. Jade kicked off her Nikes and put her food in the kitchen.

Then she went into the bedroom and changed back into her sweat shorts. "Now I'm ready," she said. Jade transferred half of the shrimp scampi onto a dinner plate, poured herself a glass of Moscato, sat down and enjoyed her dinner, alone. As Jade finished her food, her phone vibrated. *Hey baby, I'm back at the hotel. About to take a shower and lay down. Luv U, Gnite!*

Jade smiled as she read Connor's text, and texted him back: *Okay baby. Luv u 2.*

Jade poured herself another glass of Moscato and walked over to the balcony. She peeped through the semi-sheer panel and watched the rain as it pounded against the French doors.

"Guess it would be a good time to get ready for work," she said to herself.

Jade grabbed a white blouse out of the closet and a pair of gray slacks out of the drawer. She plugged in the iron and was about to turn it on when her phone rang.

"Hello. Jade?"

"This is she. Vinny?"

"No. It's Renz."

"Oh," said Jade in a surprised tone. "Why…"

"You left your credit card at the restaurant."

"Oh my goodness. I can't believe I did that," said Jade. "Thanks for calling and letting me know. I can be there in about twenty minutes."

"Have you looked outside? It's storming. We're about to close, so if you want, I can bring it to you."

"Uh, I don't know if—"

"Or you can come by tomorrow and get it," Renz interjected. "I'll lock it up for you."

Jade didn't want to go back out or stop at Vinny's tomorrow. For the next three days, she wanted to relax and enjoy her me-time.

"You know what, Renz, you can bring me my card. My address is 214 Ivory Court, apartment 2A."

"Okay. See you soon," said Renz.

Jade felt irresponsible. She couldn't believe she left her credit card at Vinny's, and then agreed to let Renz, a guy she barely knew, bring her credit card to her, at her home. What was she thinking?

Jade washed her face, brushed her teeth, and put on a pair of sweatpants. As she was putting on her sweatshirt, the doorbell rang. She opened the door, and there stood Renz, smiling.

"You're soaked," said Jade as she let Renz inside.

"I know." Renz laughed as he stepped into the apartment. "I had to park across the street and dodge a few cars."

"I'm so sorry," said Jade. "Stay right there. Let me get you a towel."

Jade shut the door and ran to the bathroom to get a towel for Renz.

Renz stood in the foyer and took off his wet sneakers. He breathed in the cashmere woods scent that filled the air. A beautiful glass-top table lined the wall. A small plant sat on top of the table, and above the table was an oval-shaped mirror framed in gold.

"Here you go," said Jade as she returned to the foyer.

"Thanks, Jade."

Renz grabbed the towel and dried his face. Then he dabbed his cornrows with the towel.

"Do you mind if I take off my socks?" he asked. "They're soaked, and I want to dry my feet."

"Not at all," replied Jade. "Go right ahead."

Renz put his socks in his sneakers and dried his feet.

"Now that we got that out of the way, we gotta do something about your clothes before you catch pneumonia," said Jade.

"And what do you suggest?"

"Follow me," replied Jade.

"Is your boyfriend here?"

"No. He's out of town," replied Jade.

Renz looked around the apartment as he followed Jade to the bathroom. He liked the apartment. The ambiance was energetic, and the decor was amazing.

He glanced at a beautiful picture of Jade and Connor on the mantel. Jade was standing in front of Connor in an elegant black gown. Connor had on a black tuxedo, and he was standing behind Jade with his arms wrapped around her waist. Jade's head was slightly turned to the left, and Connor was kissing her cheek. *What a lovely picture*, thought Renz.

"Your place is nice, Jade."

"Thanks. You can use this bathroom." Jade left Renz in the bathroom and closed the door as she exited.

"Take off your clothes," she said through the door. "I'll put them on a quick wash and dry them for you. You can wrap yourself in one of the towels on the shelf."

"My underwear too," said Renz.

"Sure, if you want them washed and dried." Jade laughed.

Renz took his wallet out of his pocket and stripped to his bare skin. He opened the door slightly and stood behind it and handed Jade his wet clothes.

"What do you want me to do now?" Renz asked.

"Are you wrapped up?" Jade asked.

"Yes." Renz laughed. "I'm all wrapped up."

"Good. Have a seat in the kitchen. I'll be right there."

Renz grabbed his wallet and opened the door. On his way to the kitchen, he stopped in the living room and admired a lovely picture of Jade sitting next to a picture of Connor. As Renz looked at Connor's picture, he noticed the diamond earing in his ear. "Whoa, that looks expensive," he whispered. Renz heard Jade's footsteps and hurried to the kitchen.

"Your clothes will be ready in about thirty minutes," she said.

"Thanks, Jade."

Jade tried not to stare but she couldn't resist. She admired his beautifully tanned skin. His chest and muscles were equally enticing. For a split second, Jade thought about giving Renz a pair of Connor's briefs, but from what she observed, Renz was bigger than Connor.

"You're not far from Vinny's at all," said Renz.

"Nope." Jade smiled.

"But I do understand why you were evasive. People are crazy. But if you got to know me, you would see that I am not crazy."

"Oh really?"

"Yes." Renz smiled.

"Do you want some tea?"

"You sure are quick to change the subject." Renz laughed. "Sure, I'll have some."

Jade heated two cups of water in the microwave. She grabbed two tea bags out of the canister and two spoons out of the drawer. She dropped one tea bag in each cup and placed the cups on the counter.

"Cream and sugar?"

"Yes," replied Renz.

Okay, so he likes his tea the same way as me, Jade said to herself. Jade put the cream and sugar on the table. Then she grabbed the cups off the counter and placed them on the table. Renz smiled as he poured the cream into his tea.

"What are you smiling at?" Jade asked.

"You," replied Renz. "I'm in awe that I'm sitting here, with you, naked and wrapped in a towel. I didn't see this coming by a long shot."

"Me either." Jade laughed.

As Jade poured cream in her tea, the glaring shine of her ring caught Renz's attention.

"Whoa! That's beautiful," yelled Renz. "When did that happen?"

"Last weekend," replied Jade as she looked at her ring.

"What a lucky guy," said Renz.

"I'm the lucky one," said Jade.

"No way, girl. He's definitely the lucky one. And that ring doesn't scare me one bit. I still want to get to know you, Jade."

"Renz, that's not possible. I'm engaged. And I'm in love with Connor."

"I know," said Renz.

"How's the tea?" Jade asked.

"Good," replied Renz. "There you go again, changing the subject. Oh, before I forget, here's your card."

"Thanks again for bringing it over," said Jade. "I really appreciate it."

"Anytime," said Renz. "What's that chiming noise?"

"The washing machine," replied Jade. "Your clothes are ready for the dryer. I'll be right back."

"Okay," said Renz.

Renz watched Jade as she walked away. He smiled to himself, still in disbelief that he was at her place, damn near naked. The thought of being alone with Jade turned him on, but Renz controlled himself.

"Okay. Your clothes are in the dryer," said Jade as she returned to the kitchen.

"Thank you so much, Jade."

"Don't mention it. So how do you like working at Vinny's?"

"I love it," replied Renz. "I'm going to own it one day."

"That's awesome, Renz. Would you hire me?"

"Nope." Renz laughed. "You're overqualified and too damn cute to be waiting tables."

Jade laughed and smiled at Renz.

"What do you do anyway?"

"I work in marketing and advertising," replied Jade.

"That sounds interesting," said Renz.

"It is," said Jade. "I meet a lot of nice people and get a lot of perks and freebies."

"Now that's a great incentive. How long have you been doing that?"

"Almost two years," replied Jade.

"Cool," said Renz.

Jade was enjoying her company and her conversation with Renz. She liked that Renz asked questions about her and didn't try to come on to her. Renz made Jade feel comfortable. So comfortable in fact, that when the timer on the dryer buzzed, Jade ignored it. She smiled at Renz, and Renz smiled at her. *What an awkward moment,* she thought.

"I think that was the dryer," said Renz.

"It was," said Jade. "Your clothes are dry. Follow me."

Renz followed Jade down the hall and to the laundry room. She took his clothes out of the dryer and handed his clothes to him.

"Nice and warm," said Renz. Renz went to the bathroom to get dressed. Afterward, he met Jade in the family room.

"Thanks for everything, Jade. I really appreciate it."

"No problem. It's the least I could do for you coming over here in a storm."

"I'd do it again," said Renz.

Renz stared into Jade's eyes. She blushed and turned away from his stare.

"I better be going," he said.

Renz followed Jade to the door. He pulled his socks out of his sneakers and realized that they were too wet to wear.

"We forgot my socks." Renz laughed. "I can't wear these," he said.

"Let me get you a bag for those," said Jade. Jade ran to the kitchen and grabbed a plastic bag out of the pantry. "Here you go."

"Thanks," said Renz.

Renz put his socks in the plastic bag. He reached for the door handle, hesitated, and turned around to face Jade.

"I could stay if you want me to," he said softly.

"That's not a good idea," said Jade. "Have a good night, Renz."

"You too, Jade."

Renz opened the door and left. Jade thought about his offer and shook her head. "Men," she whispered.

Jade looked at her ring and thought about Connor and how much she loved him. She thought about Connor's soft kisses, his gentle touch, and how good he felt inside her. Connor was all she needed.

13

Jade sat quietly in the conference room, waiting for the meeting to begin. She hoped the meeting wouldn't be long because she wasn't feeling well.

"Good morning, ladies and gentlemen," said Naomi as she entered the conference room.

"Before I get started, I just want to say that you all have been doing a really good job on your accounts. The feedback that I am receiving is outstanding. So thanks for doing what y'all do best.

"Now, more good news, we just acquired three new accounts, a skating rink, a bed and breakfast, and an adult living facility. They are all about to open within the next ninety days, so we need to get started on the marketing plans right away.

"Wade, you and your team will take the skating rink. Mimi, you got the bed and breakfast. And Sienna, you and your team will take the adult living facility. Any ideas on how we can best market these companies and help bring them some business?"

"Do they have websites and social media accounts?" Mimi asked.

"That's a great question," replied Naomi. "I'll leave that up to you all to find out."

"Okay. Then I think we should start by finding that out first," said Mimi. "Once we find that out, we'll have a better idea of what they need or lack."

"I agree," added Wade. "And we could visit the businesses and talk to the managers to get information on what their business offers."

"I like what I'm hearing guys. Anything to add, Sienna?"

"Yes. I think these businesses should offer discounts for their grand opening," replied Sienna. "Simply posting about the grand opening isn't enough. People will show up and support the business if there's something in it for them."

"I agree," said Naomi. "Okay, team leaders, I'll send your packages to you before lunch. Please disperse them to your team members. Next Friday we'll take a look at your marketing plans, so be prepared to brief me. I'll be in meetings all day, so if you need me, shoot me an e-mail."

Naomi closed her folder and walked out of the conference room. Jade and a few of her coworkers stayed in the conference room, and talked about their plans for the weekend. Jade was telling Mimi about her plans when suddenly, she grabbed her stomach and let out an agonizing cry.

"Are you okay, Jade?" Mimi asked.

"No. My stomach is killing me," replied Jade. "I'm gonna go to the bathroom."

"Okay. See you in a bit."

Jade grabbed her notebook and ran to the bathroom. As soon as she found an empty stall, she vomited.

"Oh no. This can't be good," she said.

Jade flushed the toilet and walked slowly to the sink. As she rinsed her mouth out, she realized that she had missed her cycle. Jade sprinkled a little water on her face and went back to her desk to call Connor.

"Hey, Connor."

"Jade?"

"Yeah, it's me," said Jade.

"Are you okay?" Connor asked.

"No. I just threw up," she replied.

"Aww, baby. I'm sorry you're sick. I can come get you."

"No, Connor, don't. I'll be okay."

"Are you sure?"

"Yes. I'll be fine," replied Jade.

"Okay. Feel better, baby."

"Thanks," said Jade.

Jade hung up and got back to work. By lunchtime, she felt better and decided to have lunch in the cafeteria with Mimi.

"Are you feeling better?" Mimi asked.

"Much better," replied Jade.

"Good," said Mimi. "Did you get a chance to review the information on the bed and breakfast?"

"Briefly," replied Jade. "I'll jot down some ideas this weekend."

"Great! Oh, by the way, where did Connor take you for your birthday again?"

"We went to Massanutten."

"That's right," said Mimi. "I couldn't remember the name."

"Are you going?" Jade asked.

"I might," replied Mimi. "I need a break."

Jade laughed.

"Well, it was beautiful up there. The villa was nice, and we had a lovely time."

"I bet," said Mimi. "How is Connor by the way?"

"He's good. Thanks for asking."

"No problem. Well, I'm gonna head back up. Have a nice weekend, Jade."

"You too, Mimi."

After work, Jade stopped at Walgreens to pick up a pregnancy test. She strolled down the personal care aisle and searched the net for reviews on pregnancy test products. She settled on the brand that had the most gold stars and reviews.

When Jade got home, she threw her backpack on the couch and went to the bathroom. She sat down and read the printed instructions on the back of the box. *Take the test in the morning.* She read. *Oh well,* Jade thought. *Guess this will have to wait until tomorrow.*

"Hey, Jade, I'm home," yelled Connor as he opened the door.

"I'm in here," yelled Jade.

"Are you feeling better?" Connor asked as he stepped into the bathroom.

"Yes," replied Jade.

"That's good," said Connor. "What's that?"

"A pregnancy test," replied Jade hesitantly.

"A pregnancy test! Why?"

"Because I might be pregnant," replied Jade.

"But we have been careful not to get pregnant," said Connor.

"Yes, we have. But when you came back from Charlotte, we…"

"Oh yeah, I remember," said Connor as he smiled at Jade.

Jade didn't smile back. She looked down at the box in her hand with mixed feelings, unsure if she should feel happy or sad. Even at twenty-two, Jade knew she wasn't ready for a baby. Her priority was planning her wedding, not preparing for a baby.

"So much for birth control," said Jade.

"Don't be sad," said Connor. "I want us to have a lot of kids."

"Connor, it's too soon," said Jade. "I'm not ready for a baby. We haven't even set a wedding date yet. And I have no idea how I'm going to tell my parents."

"Jade, baby, relax. First, let's find out if we're pregnant or not. Did you take the test yet?"

"No," replied Jade. "I have to take the test in the morning."

"Okay then, tomorrow it is," said Connor. "Why don't you go lay down and I'll go make you something to eat?"

"Thanks, Connor."

Connor walked Jade to the bedroom. He helped her get in bed and tucked her in. Then he went to get dinner started.

Connor poured a little oil into a skillet. He rinsed the salmon and lightly seasoned it before placing the salmon in the heated skillet. A few minutes on each side and the salmon was done. He put a bag of frozen vegetables into the microwave and pressed the express cook button.

Connor grabbed two plates out of the dishwasher, rinsed them off, dried them with a paper towel, and set them on the counter. He got a bottle of wine out of the fridge and two wineglasses out of the cabinet. Connor poured wine into his glass, and as he started to pour wine into Jade's glass, he hesitated. *If Jade is pregnant, she can't have any wine*, he thought. Connor smiled and put her glass back in the cabinet.

When the veggies were done, Connor fixed their plates and set them on the table. He lit two candles, dimmed the lights, and went to the bedroom to get Jade.

"Hey, baby, wake up," whispered Connor. "Dinner is ready."

"Not hungry," whispered Jade.

"Jade, you gotta eat something."

"Connor, I'm not hungry. Please just let me rest."

"Okay, okay. I'll put your plate in the microwave."

Connor kissed Jade and left her alone to rest. He went back into the kitchen and blew out the candles. Then he turned up the lights and sat down to eat his dinner.

After Connor ate, he took a shower and got ready for bed. His thoughts wondered to the outcome of the pregnancy test, and he prayed that the outcome would be positive.

14

It was October. Jade and Connor had another appointment with Dr. Felton. She and Connor liked Dr. Felton, and they were anxious to get a good report on baby Ellis.

"Hi, Jade," said Dr. Felton. "How are you doing?"

"Besides the morning sickness, I'm good," replied Jade.

"Well, that's usual for first time mothers. It will eventually go away. And how are you, Connor?" Dr. Felton asked.

"I'm well," replied Connor.

"That's good. Everything is going well with the baby. He or she will arrive sometime in May. I want you to start your prenatal classes soon. The classes are every Wednesday and are focused on preparing first-time mommies and daddies for their new addition. Will you be able to make the classes?"

"Absolutely," replied Connor.

"Great! I will put you two on the list. Who is your pediatrician?"

"We decided to see the doctor you recommended," replied Jade.

"Wonderful! Dr. Bennett is great. You'll like her. I think that does it for today. I want to see you next month, Jade. Please make an appointment with the receptionist on your way out."

"Thank you, Dr. Felton. I will."

After visiting with Dr. Felton, Connor headed to work, and Jade headed to Vinny's for a slice of pizza. She parked her car in front of the restaurant and went inside. Jade waved to Vinny and sat down in the first empty booth she saw.

"Well, well, well," said Renz as he sat down next to Jade. "Where have you been, gorgeous? I haven't seen you in a while."

"Busy as usual," replied Jade.

"I'd say. Everything okay?"

"Yes," replied Jade as she smiled at Renz. "How have you been?"

"Good. Could be better though."

"I see you got a new employee," said Jade.

"Yeah. That's my cousin, Lucas," said Renz. "I had to put him to work because he was getting into trouble with his no-good friends."

"What a shame. He looks like a good kid," said Jade.

"For the most part he is, but when he hangs out with his friends, the trouble begins. You took off today, huh?"

"Sure did. I had a doctor's appointment," replied Jade.

"Are you sick?"

"Yes," replied Jade.

"You're the only person I know that is happy when they're sick."

Jade laughed and said, "I'm pregnant, silly."

"What! Congratulations! You know that could've been my baby, right?"

Jade smiled at Renz. He smiled back. His statement would have been true had Jade not been in love with Connor. Jade had to admit, Renz was handsome, and if she were single, she probably would have jumped his bones.

"You're blushing," said Renz.

"And you're too much," said Jade.

"What can I get you today?"

"Just a slice of pizza and a glass of water," replied Jade.

"Cool. I'll be right back," said Renz.

Renz got up and went to the kitchen. Five minutes later, he returned with a hot slice of pizza and a glass of water.

"Here you go, Jade. Enjoy!"

"Thanks, Renz."

"You're welcome. And I took care of your bill," said Renz.

"You gotta stop doing that," she whined.

Renz smiled and walked away. Jade sat quietly and ate her pizza. When she was done, she said goodbye to Renz and went home.

* * *

When Connor arrived at his office, he got right to work making calls and responding to e-mails. As he was listening to his messages, Lisa stopped by his cubicle and interrupted him.

"And where were you this morning?" Lisa asked.

"I took Jade out for breakfast," replied Connor.

"Oh, I see," said Lisa. "Do you need help with anything today?"

"No. I got it covered," replied Connor.

"I bet you do," said Lisa. "Well, if you get backed up, just let me know. I can work overtime."

Connor shook his head and continued working. He was trying hard to stick to Nelson's plan. And for the last few months, the plan was working. Lisa only called Connor for work-related issues, and she didn't call or text Connor on his cell. Lisa had kept her promise.

But one day last week, Lisa seemed to forget her promise. She purposely bumped into Connor in the break room and smacked him on his butt.

"You got a soft ass," she said as she smiled at Connor.

Connor shook his head and walked out of the break room.

On another occasion, Lisa stopped by Connor's cubicle, wearing a skirt that fell three inches above her knees. She sat on Connor's desk and opened her legs. Connor didn't fall for the bait. He stood up and told Lisa that he was busy and that she had to go. Lisa smiled and rubbed her hand over Connor's chest before sliding off his desk and walking away.

Connor didn't say anything to Lisa, but he felt that she was beginning to overstep her boundaries, and he didn't like that feeling. Connor had to find a way to keep his distance without upsetting Lisa too much, and he had no idea how he was going to do that.

15

Jade and Connor's first Thanksgiving and Christmas in their apartment was special. For Thanksgiving, they decorated the family room in fall colors and bought a cornucopia for the table. The pumpkin, squash, and corn decor complimented the fall-colored leaves that laced the end tables.

For Christmas, Jade and Connor went to Target and purchased their first Christmas tree. They decided to buy a beautiful white Christmas tree and decorated the tree with blue and silver accessories.

Jade and Connor exchanged a few gifts, but Jade's favorite gift was the baby book for first-time mothers. Jade had a hard time putting the book down. She and Connor read the book over and over, from cover to cover.

Everything seemed to be lining up, and Jade knew it was nothing but the grace of God. However, one thing was looming, the wedding date. It hadn't been set yet.

Connor wanted to set a date right after he proposed, but Jade procrastinated. Then when Jade found out that she was pregnant, the baby became her priority. Jade told Connor that she wanted to wait until after the baby was born to get married because she wanted to look good in her wedding dress. Jade's delay bothered Connor at first, but he later accepted her wishes and didn't bring up the subject until December.

A few days after Christmas, Connor sat Jade down and had a talk with her.

"Jade, baby, it's December, and we haven't set a wedding date yet," he said. "A lot of places are going to be booked up if we keep holding off."

"You're right," said Jade. "We need to set a date. The baby is due in May, so I was thinking that maybe we can have the wedding at your parents' house during the annual cookout."

"Do you think your mom would mind?" Jade asked.

"I think she would be ecstatic," replied Connor.

"Wonderful! Then July it is," said Jade. "And I already have a wedding planner in mind."

"You do?" Connor asked surprised.

"Yep! Becca told me about some lady named Ava and that she does great work."

"Cool. Sounds like we got the hardest part taken care of already," said Connor.

"I agree," said Jade.

Becca was right. Right after the new year, Jade and Connor met with Ava Scott and she immediately got to work planning their wedding. Ava was honest and straightforward, and Jade appreciated that.

"I must warn you both," said Ava. "Time is of the essence, but I assure you that we can pull it off, and your wedding will be fabulous. First order of business is the baby. The baby is due in May, right?"

"Yes, ma'am," replied Jade.

"And the wedding date is July first?" Ava asked.

"Yes," replied Connor.

"Okay, so right after the baby is born, you're going to have to start exercising to get rid of the baby fat. We cool."

"Yes, ma'am." Jade laughed.

"Great! One of my personal trainers will contact you to start your fitness routine."

"Thank you, Ms. Scott."

"You're quite welcome! And please, call me Ava. It was a pleasure meeting you both, and I'm looking forward to working with you two. I'll be in touch."

* * *

As March rolled around, Jade was busy preparing for baby Ellis and celebrating Connor's birthday. Jade treated Connor to Nipsey's Lounge for dinner and a night of live jazz. Connor was overjoyed and had a great time celebrating his birthday with Jade and their friends. Jade gained weight and tried hard to manage it, which was hard to do because she was working from home. For Jade, the only pros to working from home were not sitting in traffic and being able to attend prenatal classes at the hospital.

Jade and Connor were overjoyed that a little Ellis baby was growing inside her belly. And in May, they were going to celebrate bringing new life into the world.

"Baby, come here," said Jade excitedly. "You gotta feel this."

Connor put his hand on Jade's stomach and felt the baby kick.

"There goes my son kicking his ass off," said Connor.

"Connor, stop with the foul language. He can hear you."

"So you think it's a boy too, huh?"

"I do," replied Jade with a smile.

"Baby, I was thinking. Can we wait until the baby is born to give it a name?"

"Sounds good to me," said Connor.

"I want the name to fit the baby. Know what I mean?"

"Girl, you're driving me crazy." Connor laughed.

"I'm sorry." Jade laughed. "Go back to what you were doing."

Aside from working all day at work, Connor had transformed his office into a nursery.

He moved his office furniture into the family room and painted the baby's room seafoam green with shades of light blue and yellow. Jade loved it. She found the cutest area rug and rocking chair online and ordered it, hoping that both items would be delivered before the baby arrived.

In April, Nelson and Marcus went to Ethan Allen with Connor to pick up the crib and the changing station Jade ordered. Afterwards, they went to Connor's house and helped him put the furniture together.

"You guys are doing such a great job," said Jade as she stood near the door to the nursery.

"Thanks, Jade," said Marcus.

"Thank you!" replied Jade. "Y'all want pizza?"

"Sure," replied Nelson.

"What toppings y'all want?"

"Sausage," replied Nelson as he smiled at Jade.

"Just cheese for me," added Marcus.

"You know how I like mine, baby."

"I sure do," said Jade as she smiled at Connor.

Jade went into the family room and called Vinny's. She placed an order for two pizzas, one with pepperoni and sausage, and one with cheese.

"Guys, the pizza will be here in forty minutes," she yelled.

"Thanks, baby," yelled Connor.

A few minutes later, the guys heard glass shatter.

"What in the world!" Connor shouted. "Be right back, fellas."

"I got it, C," said Nelson.

Nelson ran to the kitchen to help Jade. When he got there, Jade was wiping a wet substance off the counter.

"Are you okay?" Nelson asked.

"Yes. I just knocked over my glass of water," replied Jade.

"Let me clean that up for you," said Nelson.

Jade ignored Nelson and continued to clean up the mess she made.

"Jade, go sit down. I got it," said Nelson.

Nelson purposely touched Jade's hand as he reached for the towel. They stared at each other for a moment before speaking.

"What?" Jade asked as she slid her hand away from Nelson's touch.

"I owe you an apology," replied Nelson.

"An apology. For what?"

"For not being a good friend to you and Connor. Granted, I'm busy, but I should have made time to come by and see you more often. Connor is my best friend, and I would do anything for him, but I had to force myself to stay away for a while."

"Why?" Jade asked. "You know you're welcome here anytime."

"I know, but I felt myself having—"

Nelson was interrupted when Connor walked into the kitchen and wrapped his arms around Jade's stomach.

"Hey, baby, are you okay?" Connor asked as he kissed Jade on the cheek.

"Yes. Just broke another glass," replied Jade.

"Damn, baby. We're going to need another set soon."

"Boy, be quiet," said Jade. "Now what were you saying, Nelson?"

"Oh, nothing," replied Nelson. "I'm gonna go back and help Marcus. Let me know when the pizza gets here."

Nelson dropped the towel on the counter and walked out of the kitchen. He wanted to talk to Jade, but he would have to wait for the opportune time to talk to her in private.

16

Jade hadn't been feeling well, and Connor wanted to lift her spirits. Before Connor went to work, he left a sticky note for Jade on the bathroom mirror. It read, "Hey, baby. I hope you feel better today. Just hang in there, boo. We only have a few weeks to go. Have a blessed day. Luv ya." Connor hoped his note would make Jade feel better and put a smile on her face.

When Connor arrived at the office, he called Jade but got her voicemail. He left her a message and went to get a cup of coffee.

"Good morning, Connor," said Lisa as she entered the break room.

"Hey, Lisa. How are you?" Connor asked.

"Great, but I would be better if we had lunch together," replied Lisa.

"Sorry, Lisa. No can do."

"Why not?"

"You know why," said Connor. "Plus, Jade made me lunch, so I'm good."

"Yeah, right," said Lisa. "Ain't she like eight months pregnant?"

"Yeah."

"So you probably need some nook-nook," replied Lisa.

"Lisa, you can't be serious. And I thought you said you would respect my relationship with Jade."

"Yeah, I know, but that was like last year, and I still like you."

"We agreed to keep our relationship professional, but now I see that you have a different agenda. I think it would be best if you didn't say anything else to me."

"I don't think I can do that," said Lisa.

Lisa leaned her body into Connor's body and groped his penis. Connor jumped back and spilled coffee on his shirt.

"That's it! Stay the hell away from me," he shouted.

Connor stormed out of the break room and went to the bathroom to clean his shirt. When Connor returned to his desk, he called Jade.

"Hey, baby. How are you feeling?"

"Much better," replied Jade. "Thanks for the note. That was sweet."

"I'm glad you liked it."

"Are you okay? You sound a bit hyped."

"I'm fine," replied Connor.

Connor lied. He was mad and wanted to slap the hell out of Lisa, but he didn't hit girls. He also wanted to tell Jade what happened, but telling Jade would upset her and that wouldn't be good for her or the baby.

"How's baby Ellis doing?" Connor asked

"Fine. I think he's ready to join us," replied Jade.

"Soon enough, baby. I'll stop by the store and pick up the baby favors after work. Did you order the chicken?"

"Oh shoot. Thanks for reminding me," replied Jade.

"What do you want for dinner?"

"Jamaican food," replied Jade.

"Okay. I'll pick that up too. Hey, I gotta go see my uncle. Talk to you later. Love you."

"Okay, baby. Love you too."

Connor hung up the phone and went to his uncle's office. His uncle didn't tolerate any form of harassment, including sexual, and such behavior had to be reported. Connor knocked on the door as he stepped inside the office. "Excuse me, Uncle Greg, can I talk to you for a minute?"

"Sure," replied Greg. "What is it?"

"I have a personal issue with an employee," replied Connor.

"Shut the door and have a seat," said Greg.

Connor shut the door and sat down in the leather chair in front of the desk. He looked at his uncle and said, "Lisa touched me inappropriately, and I don't feel comfortable working with her."

"Can you be more specific?" Greg asked.

As Connor shared the details with Greg, his face became masked with shock.

"She did what!" Greg shouted. "When did this happen?"

"This morning, before you got here," replied Connor.

"Do you want to file a formal complaint?"

"No," replied Connor. "But can you talk to her or move her to another section?"

"I will have a talk with her," replied Greg.

"Thank you, sir."

"And how is my niece doing?"

"She's doing well," replied Connor. "Thanks for asking."

Connor left Greg's office and returned to his desk. He realized he left his coffee in the break room and went to get it. When Connor entered the break room, he saw Malcolm sitting at the table.

"Hey, Connor. What's up, man?" Malcolm asked.

"Hey, Malcolm."

"Was that you I heard shouting earlier?"

"Yeah, man. That girl won't leave me alone," replied Connor.

"What girl are you talking about?"

"I'd rather not say," replied Connor.

"Man, I have a pretty good idea of who you're talking about," said Malcolm. "We all see how she looks at you, how she's always at your desk. She got people in the office thinking y'all dating. Be careful, man."

Malcolm left Connor in the break room. Connor dumped his coffee in the sink and poured himself a fresh cup.

He went back to his desk and called a few staging and site managers. By the time he was done making his calls, it was eleven thirty. Connor went downstairs to get a sandwich. As Connor ordered his sandwich, his phone vibrated. *You son of a bitch, you got me fired. I will make you pay for this, just watch!*

"This girl is crazy," Connor said to himself. Connor was thrilled that Lisa was gone. He took a breath of relief and paid for his food.

Back at his desk, there was a note on his computer. It read, *Come see me. Greg.* Connor took a bite of his sandwich and went to Greg's office.

"Yes, Uncle Greg," said Connor.

"Close the door and have a seat," said Greg.

Connor heard the seriousness in his uncle's voice. He shut the door and sat down.

"Listen, I had to let Lisa go," said Greg. "And there may be an investigation."

"An investigation. Why? I said that I didn't want to file a formal complaint."

"I know, but Lisa made a few accusations as well."

"Accusations?" Connor said. "What do you mean?"

"She said that you asked her to touch you, that you two are seeing each other, and that you promised her that you were going to leave Jade."

"What the hell! That bitch is crazy!" yelled Connor.

"She may be," added Greg. "Lisa threatened the company as well. She said she was going to file assault charges on you and the company, and that's when I decided to fire her. I must warn you that if Lisa decides to make any claims against you or the company, true or false, there will be an investigation."

"What!" Connor shouted. "I don't need this shit, Uncle Greg. My life is perfect right now, and that crazy bitch is trying to…"

"Calm down, Connor," said Greg. "I'm sure everything will be fine."

Connor was furious and couldn't contain his anger. He jumped up in a rage and balled his hands into fists as he paced the floor.

"I'm gonna fuck her up," Connor said.

"Are you out of your mind, boy? You will do no such thing. You're going to sit your ass down and calm down. I want you to go home and relax, and this discussion stays right here, got it?"

"Yes, sir."

When Connor was calm, he left his uncle's office and went home. He stopped at the store and picked up the baby shower favors and a beautiful bouquet of flowers for Jade. Connor was a block away from home when he realized he forgot to get Jade's food. "Damn it," he yelled to himself. Lisa's actions and threats distracted him. Connor made a U-turn and headed to the Jamaican restaurant.

Jade was lounging on the couch when Connor got home. Connor put the food and the baby favors in the kitchen. Then he went into the family room to give Jade her flowers.

"You're home early," said Jade.

"These are for you," said Connor.

"Oh, baby, thank you. They're beautiful."

Jade sat up to admire her flowers and then she gave Connor a kiss.

"Let me put them in water right now," she said.

"Are you feeling better?"

"Yes," replied Jade. "Thanks for picking up the favors and dinner. The food smells delicious. Are you ready to eat?"

Connor didn't answer.

"Baby, are you ready to eat?"

Connor was silent. He stared inattentively at the television, still distracted by what happened at work. As Jade massaged her stomach, she walked over to Connor and stood in front of him.

"Connor. Connor," she repeated. "What's going on? Didn't you hear me?"

"Sorry, baby," replied Connor. "What did you say?"

"Are you ready to eat?"

"No. I'm not hungry," he replied.

Jade sat down next to Connor. Her intuition told her something was wrong, and she wanted to help him. She had never seen Connor like this before, and it bothered her.

"Baby, what's wrong? Whatever it is, it's clearly affecting you. You can talk to me, Connor, I'm right here," said Jade.

Connor looked at Jade with a bleak smile.

"I know, baby," he said. "I'm gonna go lay down for a while."

Jade felt sad for Connor but there was nothing she could do if he didn't want to talk. Jade watched Connor as he walked away. When he was out of her view, she went to the kitchen and made herself a plate of Jamaican food. After Jade ate, she went to the bedroom to check on Connor. Connor was lying on his back with one arm resting on his forehead and his other arm resting over his stomach.

Jade watched Connor for a minute. She thought he looked sexy lying in bed with his briefs on. Jade turned on the television to the Slow Jams channel and crawled in bed with Connor.

Jade moved Connor's arm and kissed his forehead. Then she kissed the side of Connor's face until she reached his lips and gave him a passionate tongue kiss. Without saying a word, Connor turned Jade on her side, pulled down her shorts and panties, and entered her from behind.

"Ahh," he whispered. "You feel so nice and warm."

As the music played in the background, Connor and Jade made love to one another.

17

Tears rolled down Jade's face as the people she loved and cared about arrived to celebrate the upcoming birth of baby Ellis. Her mom and dad were there, Zaria was there, her cousin Sydney was there, and her besties Sophia and Becca were there too. Jade was happy to see Alexa and a few of her coworkers, including her supervisor, Naomi.

"I appreciate y'all for coming," said Jade. "It really means a lot."

"Girl, we weren't going to miss your baby shower for anything," said Mimi.

"Thanks, Mimi," said Jade.

"We really miss your smiling face at the office," said Naomi.

"I miss you guys too," cried Jade. "Hopefully, I'll be back soon."

Everyone ate and drank until their hearts were content. After dinner, Sophia and Becca helped Jade with her gifts. Jade was excited to see all the nice gifts for the baby, and she couldn't wait to put them to use. Her parents bought her a lovely car seat and baby carrier set. Jade loved it.

"Guys, thank y'all so much," said Jade. "I have no idea where I'm going to put all this stuff."

"Well, at least you got a place to put the clothes," said Alexa.

"I sure do," said Jade.

"You can leave the bigger items in here," said Sydney.

"Right here in the family room?" Jade asked.

"Sure, why not," replied Sydney. "There's space near Connor's desk to stack them up."

"That's a good idea," said Jade. "Thanks Sydney."

"No problem, cuz," said Sydney.

"Whatever you don't want, I'll take," shouted Zaria.

"Are you trying to tell me something?" Jade's mother asked.

"Not yet Mom," replied Zaria.

"What did Connor's parents get the baby?" Sophia asked.

"A stroller," replied Jade. "I hope it gets here before the baby."

"Did you and Connor decide on a name?" Becca asked.

"Not yet. We want to wait until baby Ellis is born," replied Jade.

"Cool. I know y'all will come up with a nice name," said Becca.

As the baby shower ended, Jade hugged her guests and handed them a baby-shower favor as they left. Her parents, Zaria, and Sydney stayed a while longer to help clean up and store her gifts away.

"The baby shower was beautiful," said Jade. "Thank y'all so much. Y'all really outdid yourselves."

"You know we got you girl," said Zaria.

"Thanks, sis. Ooh, let me call Connor and tell him how nice everything was."

"Hey, baby," said Jade.

"Hey. How's the baby shower going?"

"Great," replied Jade. "We're finishing up now. Baby Ellis got some really nice gifts. I can't wait for you to see them."

"I'll see them when I get home," said Connor.

"Are you on your way?"

"No. I'm gonna stay here a little while longer," replied Connor.

"Okay. Well, tell Nelson I said hello. See ya when you get here."

"Okay, baby," said Connor.

After Jade's family cleaned up the house, they said their good-byes and headed home. Jade went into the nursery and looked at the baby gifts. As she was admiring the cute little onesies, she heard the front door open. "Daddy's home," she whispered.

Connor walked into the family room and saw the boxes piled up near his desk. He smiled and shook his head.

"Jade, I'm home," he yelled.

"I'm in the nursery," shouted Jade.

Connor joined Jade in the nursery. They kissed and looked around the room, admiring Connor's paint job. Jade was overjoyed that the rocking chair and area rug had finally arrived. She pictured herself rocking the baby to sleep in that chair, and she couldn't wait to make it a reality.

"Didn't the nursery come out beautiful?"

"It sure did," replied Connor. "Now what are we going to do when baby number two comes?"

"Number two! Number one isn't even here yet." Jade laughed.

Connor leaned down and kissed Jade's belly. She was huge, but to Connor, she was beautiful.

"Hey, baby Ellis. It's your daddy," said Connor. "You gotta hurry up and come so Mommy and Daddy can get started on a baby sister for you."

"Connor, you're crazy," said Jade.

18

It was a beautiful Saturday in May. Jade and Connor woke up early and went to the park for a walk. Kids were running around, screaming, climbing up the slide, and swinging on the swings. Jade smiled as she thought of swinging on the swings and sliding down the slide with her baby.

"Penny for your thoughts," Connor said.

"I was just thinking about you pushing me and the baby on the swing."

"Oh, I'm the pusher, huh?"

"Absolutely," replied Jade as she smiled at Connor.

Jade and Connor sat down on the bench and watched the kids as they played tag. Watching the little boys chase the little girls around the park fueled Jade's excitement. She looked forward to the following week for so many reasons. It was her due date, her mother was driving up from Southampton to help with the baby, and Connor was transitioning to a work-from-home schedule.

When Jade got up from the bench, she felt wet. She looked at Connor, and Connor looked at her.

"What's wrong, baby?"

"My water broke," replied Jade.

"Really," shouted Connor. "Let's go."

Connor helped Jade to the apartment. He sat her down on the couch and ran to the bedroom to get the camcorder and Jade's backpack. He grabbed his car keys, helped Jade up from the couch, and headed out the door.

Connor rushed Jade to the hospital. He double-parked outside the emergency room and ran inside the hospital to get help. Within minutes, Connor and a nurse pushing a wheelchair ran outside. Connor helped the nurse get Jade out of the car and into the wheelchair. The nurse rolled Jade into the emergency room while Connor parked the car. As Connor ran back toward the hospital, his phone vibrated. "Who the hell is texting me?" he said.

I see you're busy now, but don't worry. I will get you!

Connor ignored Lisa's text. He put his phone in his pocket and went inside the hospital to find Jade.

"Excuse me. I'm looking for Jade Simpson," said Connor.

"And you are?" the nurse asked suspiciously.

"Connor Ellis, her fiancé," he replied.

"Follow me. I'll take you to her," said the nurse. The nurse led Connor down the corridor and to a small triage room.

"Here she is, Mr. Ellis."

"Thank you," said Connor.

Connor walked over to Jade and gave her a kiss. "How are you feeling?" he asked, almost breathless.

"I'm good," replied Jade. "But I think you should sit down and catch your breath." Jade laughed.

Connor sat down and grabbed Jade's hand. "Where is Dr. Felton?" he asked.

"She's on her way down," replied Jade.

"Cool," said Connor. "I think baby Ellis is ready to come."

"Me too," said Jade. "Can you get my phone out of my backpack? I need to call my parents."

Jade called her mother and left a message that she and Connor were at the hospital and that they needed to get to the hospital as soon as possible.

"Well, hello, Jade," said Dr. Felton as she entered the room. "How are you feeling?"

"Okay," replied Jade. "I think it's time though."

"Let me take a look at you," said Dr. Felton.

Dr. Felton gently pressed her fingers around Jade's expanded stomach and timed her contractions.

"Ms. Jade?"

"Yes, Doctor."

"It's time to get you prepped. Looks like baby Ellis is ready to join us. The nurses will be right in to take you and Connor upstairs to delivery. See you both in a few minutes."

"Thanks, Dr. Felton," said Connor.

Connor looked at Jade and said, "You and the baby are the most important things in my life, Jade. I don't know what I would do without you two."

"We love you too, Connor. Did you call your parents?"

"Yes. They're flying up in the morning," he replied.

"I sent Sophie and Becca a text. They're on their way. What about Nelson and Marcus?"

"I left them messages," replied Connor.

The nurses entered the room and took Jade and Connor upstairs to the maternity ward. In the birthing room, one of the nurses helped Jade undress and put on a hospital gown. The other nurse helped Connor put on hospital scrubs.

Dr. Felton entered the room in her scrubs, ready to go to work.

"Okay people, here we go," said Dr. Felton. "Let's do this!"

Connor grabbed Jade's hand and gave her a kiss. Jade tightened her grip and smiled at Connor as a tear rolled down her face.

With every contraction, Jade screamed and squeezed Connor's hand. She was in pain, but she knew it was worth it. Her bundle of joy would soon be arriving.

"Push, Jade," said the doctor. "Breathe. You're doing great. Don't push yet. Okay, push. Very good! You're doing wonderful. Breathe, push, relax, breathe, push, relax," uttered Dr. Felton.

"So many instructions." Jade laughed as she looked at Connor.

"You're doing great, baby, but you're crushing my fingers," joked Connor.

"Sorry, baby, but it hurts," cried Jade.

"It'll be over soon," said Connor. "I promise."

"I see the head," said the doctor. "You're doing great, Jade."

"Baby, I need my hand now so I can record this."

Jade let go of Connor's hand. Connor grabbed the camcorder and stood near the doctor to record the baby's birth. Through the lens, Connor saw the crown of the baby's head; he saw how gentle and careful Dr. Felton was as she freed the baby from Jade's body. And then the baby was in the doctor's hands, wailing.

"It's a girl," yelled Dr. Felton.

Jade was ecstatic. Tears rolled down Jade's face as she heard her baby girl cry for the first time.

Connor recorded Dr. Felton cut the umbilical cord and hand the baby to the nurse. He recorded the nurse clean the fluid from the baby's nose and mouth and wrap the baby in a blanket. Connor followed the nurse to Jade's bedside and recorded the nurse as she placed baby Ellis in Jade's arms.

He moved closer to the bed to get a close-up of Jade and the baby. Connor's first video of his baby girl had to be perfect.

"Connor, she's beautiful," said Jade.

"Just like her mom," Connor commented.

Connor stopped recording and sat down next to Jade.

"She's gorgeous," whispered Connor. "So what are we going to name her?"

"She looks like a Jordan to me," replied Jade. "What do you think?"

"Jordan Marie Ellis. I love it."

"Me too! Here, Connor, hold your daughter."

Connor held Jordan for a few minutes before the nurse took her away.

"Will you be breastfeeding, dear?" the nurse asked.

"Yes, ma'am," replied Jade in a drained tone.

"Great! I'll go dress your baby and bring her back for her first feeding."

"Thank you very much," replied Jade as she closed her eyes.

"Baby, get some rest. I'll go see if your parents are here."

"Okay, Connor. Hurry back," said Jade.

"I will," said Connor.

Connor entered the waiting room and saw Jade's parents and his friends, sitting together and talking like they were college kids. When Jade's mother saw Connor, she rushed to him in tears and gave him a hug. Jade's father shook Connor's hand and gave him a cigar.

"How is Jade doing?" Tanya asked.

"She's doing well," replied Connor. "She'll be in a private room soon, and then we can go see her and Jordan."

"My first grandson," yelled Louis. "I know he's as handsome as his granddaddy."

"He's a she, Mr. Simpson." Connor laughed.

"What!" Mr. Simpson yelled.

"That is a lovely name," said Tanya.

"Congratulations, bro. You're a daddy now," said Nelson. "I know my niece is beautiful."

"She's adorable," said Connor. "Wait until you see her."

Connor sat down with Jade's parents. He told them how well the birth went and that Jade was a real trooper.

Thirty minutes later, a nurse entered the waiting room and told Connor that Jade had been moved to a private room. Everyone stood up, ready to see Jade and the baby.

"Sorry, only immediate family can see her now," said the nurse as she held up her hand.

"What about my friends?" Connor asked. "They want to see the baby."

"They will have to see the baby in the nursery," replied the nurse. "Sorry, but that's our policy."

"I understand," said Connor. "Guys, I'm sorry. I didn't know."

"It's okay, Connor. We'll wait to see Jordan in the nursery," said Becca.

Connor, Tanya, and Louis followed the nurse to Jade's room. Jade had just finished feeding Jordan when her family entered the room.

"Mom, Dad, come meet Jordan Marie Ellis."

Jade's parents gathered around the bed, admiring their first grandchild.

"She's adorable," said Tanya.

"Yes, she is," said Louis. "You did good, Jade. She's beautiful."

As Jade's mother rocked Jordan in her arms, Connor grabbed his camcorder and recorded the intimate moment.

"This video is gonna be awesome," said Connor.

"Not if you're not in it," said Louis. "Hold Jordan and let me record you with your family."

As Connor held Jordan, her little pink lips opened to a yawn. Her tiny eyes opened for a split second and then they closed.

"Hey, Jordan. This is your daddy talking," said Connor. "I want you to know that I love you. I have so many things to teach you, so many stories to share with you, and so many kisses to give you. And I promise to be the best father a little girl could ever have."

Connor sealed his promise with a kiss to Jordan's tiny cheek.

* * *

Jade barely slept. She thought about Jordan all night and wanted to hold her. She looked at Connor, who was sleeping in the chair.

"Connor, Connor," she yelled. "Wake up. I want to see Jordan."

Connor slowly opened his eyes, looked at Jade and asked, "What was that baby?"

"I want to see Jordan," she repeated.

"Baby, the nurse will bring her in soon."

"Well, I think she may be hungry," said Jade.

"Okay. Let me go get the nurse."

As Connor walked to the door, his parents walked in the room holding balloons and a stuffed animal for Jordan.

"Mom, Dad," yelled Connor as he hugged his parents. "Y'all made it. When did y'all get here?"

"About an hour ago," replied his mother. "You and Jade were sleeping, so we went to the nursery to see the baby. She's gorgeous, Connor."

"Thanks," said Connor. "Come and see Jade. She just woke up, but I know she'll be glad to see y'all. I'll be right back."

"Okay, baby," said his mother.

Connor left the room and headed to the nursery. Gordon and Julia made their way to Jade's bedside.

"How are you doing, Jade?" Julia asked.

"Tired." Jade laughed.

"I bet you are," said Julia. "Jade, the baby is beautiful, just beautiful."

"Thank you. And thank you both for coming. It means a lot," said Jade as she closed her eyes.

"Get some rest, sweetie. Gordon and I are going to check in at the hotel, and then we'll come back to see you, okay."

"Okay, Mrs. Ellis," said Jade. "Thanks again for coming. See y'all later."

19

At two weeks old, Jordan was the center of everyone's attention. When Jade wasn't resting, she was with Jordan, which meant that she didn't get much done around the house. Thank goodness her mother was there. Jade's mother stayed with her and Connor for a few weeks after Jordan was born. Having two kids of her own, she knew Jade would need some time to adjust to her life as a new mother.

Connor and Tanya took care of everything while Jade rested and took care of Jordan. Connor did most of the cooking and when he had a few hours to spare, he helped Tanya with the domestic chores.

Most days, Connor would find Jade in the nursery, rocking Jordan in the rocking chair. And every time Connor saw Jade and Jordan, he would rush to the bedroom and get the camcorder.

Today was no different. Connor stood in the doorway of the nursery and recorded his girls as he narrated.

"And here are my two favorite girls, Ms. Jade and little Ms. Jordan," said Connor. "Your daddy is gonna spoil you, baby girl."

"Are you making another video?"

"Absolutely," replied Connor. "And I am calling it *My Two Girls*."

"You're so silly," said Jade.

When Jordan fell asleep, Jade put her in the crib, covered her with a blanket, and kissed her on the cheek. And Connor got it all on tape.

"You can stop recording now," said Jade.

"Wait. Smile," said Connor. "Your smile will be the perfect ending to my video."

Connor watched Jade through the lens as she foolishly smiled into the camcorder. Then Jade made a funny face and stuck out her tongue. Connor laughed and stopped the recording.

"You're so beautiful, Jade."

With his free hand, he grabbed Jade and kissed her on the lips. Jade wrapped her arms around Connor's neck and kissed him back. Then she opened her mouth and put her tongue in his mouth. They tongue kissed until they were interrupted.

"Jade, sweetie," yelled her mother.

"Coming," yelled Jade.

"Jordan is finally asleep," said Jade as she sat down next to her mother.

"You know, Jade, it's best to rest when the baby rests."

"I know Ma, but I'm not tired. And plus, you're here."

"Oh no, I spoiled you." Tanya laughed.

"You and Mrs. Ellis have been a great help, Mom. I'm so glad you both were here. I still can't believe y'all watched the video four times."

"It was amazing to see Jordan enter the world," said Tanya.

"Yes, it was," said Connor. "I think you should take your mom's advice and rest. I'll start dinner and come get you when it's ready."

"Okay, I'll go rest."

In the bedroom, Jade closed the curtains to block out the light that seeped through the blinds. Then she slid under the covers and rested.

"What are you making?" Tanya asked as she joined Connor in the kitchen.

"Baked fish, sautéed kale, and roasted red potatoes," replied Connor.

"Now that sounds delicious!"

"I think you'll like it, Mrs. Simpson."

"Connor, I think it would be fine if you called me Tanya. I mean, we're practically family now."

"Okay, Ms. Tanya," said Connor. "You want some wine?"

"Sure," replied Tanya.

Connor reached for a wineglass in the cabinet and poured Tanya a glass of wine.

"I want to thank you, Connor," she said.

"Ma'am?"

"For taking care of my Jade. You're doing a great job."

"Thank you," said Connor. "I love Jade, Ms. Tanya."

"I can see that," said Tanya.

"How much longer can you stay?" Connor asked.

"Probably another day or two," replied Tanya. "I gotta get back home, take care of my husband, and check on the stores."

"I know what you mean," said Connor. "I go back in the office next week. My uncle said, '*Two weeks at home is all you get, boy.*'"

"Well, it sure is nice that you both can work from home. We didn't have that option back in my day," said Tanya.

"It is. Jade will be working from home for another two months, which is awesome. We'll be married by then and back from our honeymoon. I hate to cut the conversation short, but I gotta go check on my girls and get back to work. Do you need anything?"

Tanya shook her head from left to right. Connor went to the bedroom to check on Jade. She was resting comfortably. He leaned down and gave Jade a kiss. Then he went to check on Jordan. She looked like an angel. Connor leaned over the crib railing and gave Jordan a kiss. As Connor made his way back to the family room, his phone vibrated. *I'm on my way over to bring my goddaughter a gift.*

Connor turned on his laptop and got to work. He responded to a few e-mails and accepted meeting invites that pertained to him. When the doorbell rang, Tanya glanced over at Connor, who was focused on his work.

"I'll get it," said Tanya. "Tend to your work, honey."

"Thank you, Ms. Tanya."

Tanya opened the door and saw Nelson standing in the doorway. He was smiling and holding a small gift bag.

"Oh, hi there," said Tanya. "Nelson, right?"

"Yes, ma'am," replied Nelson.

"Well, come on in," said Tanya as she smiled at Nelson.

"Thank you," said Nelson as he entered the apartment.

"Hey, C, what's up?" Nelson asked.

"Hey, man," replied Connor. "Just finished working. And you're right on time for dinner."

"Not hungry," said Nelson. "I just left the gym and wanted to drop off a gift for Jordan."

"That's sweet of you," said Tanya. "Let me take that. And I'll go wake Jade. I'm sure she'll want to thank you."

"Thank you," said Nelson.

Nelson followed Connor to the kitchen and watched him as he set the table and lit the candles.

"Look at you, C. All romantic and shit," said Nelson.

"Jade loves candles man," said Connor.

"How's work and you know who?"

"Man, I have been so busy with the baby and planning the wedding that I forgot to tell you the latest about her," replied Connor.

Connor walked over to Nelson and showed him Lisa's texts.

"Whoa! Man, she got issues. These are threats, C. You need to keep these."

"No way. I'm deleting all her shit," said Connor.

"What the hell happened?" Nelson asked. "I thought the working relationship was on the up and up."

"It was for a while," replied Connor. "Then last month she got out of control, and my uncle fired her crazy ass."

Nelson shook his head. As Connor started to delete the texts, Jade walked into the kitchen and interrupted him. Connor quickly put his phone down on the table. He looked at Nelson and put his index finger up to his lips, signaling Nelson to be quiet.

"Hey, Nelson. How you doing?" Jade asked.

"Good," he replied.

"Thanks for the stuffed animal," said Jade. "Jordan is going to love it."

"Don't mention it," said Nelson.

Nelson watched Jade as she walked over to Connor and rubbed his back with her hand.

"Dinner smells delicious," said Jade.

"Thanks baby," said Connor as he planted a kiss on Jade's cheek.

"Well, guys, I gotta get going," said Nelson. "C, I'll get with you later."

"Why don't you stay for dinner?" Jade asked.

"Maybe next time," replied Nelson.

Nelson got up from the kitchen table and walked to the door.

"Let me walk you out," said Jade. "And thanks for stopping by. It's always good to see you."

"Same here," said Nelson. Nelson turned around and smiled at Jade.

"Smiling hard, I see. Who's the lucky girl?"

Nelson didn't respond. He stared at Jade for a minute before he hugged her. As Nelson disengaged, he kissed Jade on her lips. Jade was shocked. She took a step back and looked at Nelson with a perplexed gaze on her face.

"Nelson, what are you doing?"

"I can't stop thinking…"

"Good night," said Jade.

Nelson opened the door and let himself out. Jade locked the door and joined her family for dinner.

Jade was quiet at the dinner table. She fiddled with her fork and stared at her food.

"You okay, Jade?" her mother asked.

"Yeah, I'm good," she replied.

"I guess she's not hungry," said Connor.

After dinner, Connor and Tanya cleaned up the kitchen. When they were done, Tanya went to Jade's bedroom to rest, Connor sat in the family room and watched television, and Jade warmed up a bottle of breast milk to feed Jordan.

Jordan looked into her mother's eyes as Jade rocked her in the rocking chair. Jade pulled her phone out of her pocket to take a picture of Jordan and saw a text from Nelson.

> *Jade, I apologize for making you feel uncomfortable. That was not my intent. But I will not apologize for kissing you. I know that doesn't make sense when it was my kiss that made you feel uncomfortable, but what else can I say. I hope you can forgive me.*

20

As the days passed, Jade got excited about waking up to see Jordan and dress her in her cute little outfits. Connor couldn't wait to get home from work and finalize their wedding plans.

Ava was a huge help. Ava helped Jade and Connor with everything from the flower arrangements to the hotel reservations.

But there was still a lot more to do.

Jade wanted lighted floating flower petals in the pool, an ice sculpture, tents for eating, and a never-ending juice fountain, and Ava was coming over to Jade's house to help her decide.

Jade jumped with excitement when she heard the doorbell.

"Hi, Ava," said Jade. "Come in."

"Hello, Jade," said Ava.

"Let's sit in the family room," said Jade. "Would you like something to drink?"

"Sweet tea would be fine," replied Ava.

"Coming right up," said Jade.

Ava sat down in the family room and waited for Jade to return. She took out her planning book and her supply catalog and placed them on the table.

"I think we're right on target," said Jade as she handed Ava a glass of tea.

"Thank you," said Ava.

"I sent my family the wedding invitations through WedEvites and most of them responded that they will be attending. So that's a total of fifty invites, but like a hundred and fifty people." Jade laughed.

"Awesome!" Ava exclaimed. "I reserved twenty rooms at the Hilton, but I think you're going to need more. I'll call the hotel and get that taken care of. Now, the closest Hilton to your future in-laws is thirty minutes away. Do you think your family would be okay with that?"

"They'll have to be," replied Jade.

"Who's officiating the wedding?"

"Connor's pastor," replied Jade.

"Good," said Ava. "Here's pictures of the flower arrangements and the lighted floating flower petals. Do you like?"

"Ava, they're gorgeous," replied Jade. "How did you get white and lilac flower petals?"

"I have my sources," replied Ava. "Go ahead and pick out the tents and the ice sculpture, and I will finalize the contracts later this week. Now all I need is for you and Connor to decide on the wedding cake and the juice fountain. I'll need that info as soon as possible."

"We'll have that info by next week," said Jade.

"Now, did you find a dress? And have you and Connor decided on the wedding songs?"

"Yes, I found a dress," replied Jade.

Jade picked up her cell phone and showed Ava a sexy V-neck backless dress.

"Beautiful! That is going to look stunning on you," said Ava. "And the songs?"

"We haven't decided yet, but I promise you we will have the songs by the time we see you again."

"Okay. I need the father-daughter song as well," said Ava.

"Shoot, I completely forgot about that," said Jade. "I'll check with my dad and get back to you."

"Great! How is my personal trainer working out for ya?"

"Renard is awesome," replied Jade. "And I appreciate him coming in the evening when Connor is home. He put me on a twice-a-week program."

"Told ya he was good," said Ava. "And how is Jordan doing?"

"Fine," replied Jade. "All she does is sleep. Do you want to see her?"

"No, it's okay," replied Ava. "Let her sleep. I'll see her next time. Where are you and Connor going for the honeymoon?"

"Bora Bora. Neither one of us have been there before, so we are really looking forward to it."

"That sounds lovely, Jade. Oh, I spoke with Mrs. Ellis yesterday and gave her an update. She is so excited for you and Connor. I can't wait to meet her."

"You're going to love her. She's sweet," Jade commented.

"Well, I think that about covers it," said Ava. "Thanks for the tea, and tell Connor I said hello."

"I will, Ava. Thanks so much for everything."

"You bet," said Ava.

21

Jordan's appointment with Dr. Bennett went well. Jade informed Dr. Bennett that Jordan was eating well but slept a lot. Dr. Bennett laughed and told Jade not to worry, that's normal. Jordan is fine and growing right on schedule. She also told Jade that she wanted to see Jordan in three months. Jade was okay with that because by then, she and Connor would be married and back from their honeymoon.

When they got home, Jade fed Jordan and put her to sleep. Then she helped Connor pack for his business trip. Jade hated that Connor had to travel so soon after Jordan was born, but she knew he had work to do.

"Hey, baby, I found that blue tie you were looking for. Do you want to take it with you?"

"No. I'm gonna take a different one," replied Connor.

"So you'll be back Friday, right?"

"Yeah, and I plan to spend the weekend with my two favorite girls," replied Connor.

"You know, we can just go with you," said Jade.

"It's too soon for Jordan to be traveling," said Connor.

"Well, then I guess we'll see you Friday," said Jade.

Connor heard his phone vibrate. He picked up his phone and read the text. *Payback is a bitch!*

Instantly, Connor's demeanor changed. He tried to hide his agitation, but Jade noticed.

"What's wrong?" Jade asked.

"Nothing," replied Connor.

"Was that Uncle Greg?"

"No. That was Nelson bothering me again. I gotta find him a girl." Connor laughed.

"I agree," said Jade.

"Will you do me a favor and have Sophie and Becca come over? I would feel better if your girls were here with you and Jordan."

"Connor, we'll be fine. They do have jobs, ya know."

"I know, but I would feel better if they were here with you."

"Okay, okay," said Jade. "I'll call them and see when they can come over."

"Thank you. I have a few minutes before I hit the road," said Connor.

Connor crawled over to Jade and kissed her. Between the kissing and moaning, they took off their clothes and got under the covers. Connor got on top of Jade and kissed her neck, then he kissed her breasts and her nipples.

"I can't get enough of you girl," whispered Connor. "You always make me feel better. *Ti amo*."

When Connor entered Jade, she let out a gratifying sigh and closed her eyes as Connor made love to her.

* * *

By Wednesday, Jade was bored and lonely. Friday was too far away. Jade missed Connor, and she wanted him home. But Jade had something to look forward to. Sophia and Becca had accepted her invitation and were stopping by to see her and Jordan after work.

Jade was elated when Sophia and Becca arrived. Sophia and Becca played with Jordan and took lots of pictures with her.

"So how do you like Ava?" Becca asked.

"She's wonderful," replied Jade. "Thanks for the recommendation."

"Told ya," said Becca.

After playtime with Jordan, Jade and her friends had a few drinks and played cards all night. At midnight Jade kicked her friends out of her house and went to bed.

Jade woke up late Thursday morning. She was tired and had a hard time getting herself on track. Everything was off; Jordan's feeding, her nap, her wash down, everything. She innocently blamed Sophia and Becca for keeping her up late.

After Jade fed Jordan and put her to sleep, she took a quick shower. Then she got dressed, logged onto her laptop, and sent Mimi an e-mail. Three unanswered e-mails were in Jade's inbox awaiting her response. After Jade responded to the e-mails, she checked her phone and realized she missed two calls from Connor.

Jade toasted two pieces of wheat bread and added a spoonful of avocado spread to each slice. She called Connor back but got his voicemail, so she left him a message: *Morning, baby, it's me and Jordan. Sorry we missed your calls. I overslept. We miss you very much, and we can't wait to see you tomorrow. Love you.*

After Jade ate, she got back to work. During her down time, she cleaned the house and prepped Jordan's bottles.

At four-thirty, Jade logged off her computer, dressed Jordan in a cute baby jumper and took her to the park. The evening air felt good to Jade as she strolled Jordan through the park. After their brief walk, Jade sat on the swing and held Jordan tight as she slowly rocked back and forth, making sure her feet stayed on the ground. She took a few selfies with Jordan and sent them to Connor, with the caption, "We miss you."

When Jade got home, she opened the balcony doors to let the evening air flow into the house. Then she strapped Jordan into her rocker and played with her. After playtime, Jade brought Jordan in the bathroom with her while she took a shower. After Jade showered, she fed Jordan and laid Jordan in her crib, but Jordan wouldn't go to sleep. Jade rocked Jordan in the rocking chair for thirty minutes before she fell asleep, then she put Jordan down in her crib and made herself something to eat. After Jade ate, she went to bed.

Twenty-minutes later, Jade was awakened by Jordan's cry. She ran into Jordan's room and picked her up, and cradled Jordan in her arms until she stopped crying. Jade looked into Jordan's beautiful eyes; she was wide awake.

"Little one," she said, *"you gotta go back to sleep because Mommy has to get some rest."*

Jordan smiled as she looked up at her mother.

Maybe she's tired of that crib, Jade thought. Jade brought Jordan into her bedroom and laid her down on the bed. She turned on the television, and climbed in the bed with Jordan. Then she checked her phone and realized she missed Connor's call. Jade muted the television and called Connor back.

"Hey," said Jade.

"Hey, sweetie," said Connor. "Where have you been?"

"I woke up late, and my whole day was off," said Jade. "Then after work, I took Jordan to the park. She liked it."

"I see. I'm looking at the pictures now," said Connor. "I wish I were there with y'all."

"We do too."

"Why are you up so late?"

"Your daughter is wide awake," replied Jade. "I think she wants you to put her to sleep."

"Put the phone on speaker so she can hear my voice," said Connor.

"Okay, you're on speaker," said Jade.

"Hey, my little bambina. It's Daddy. I'll be home tomorrow. Daddy misses you and loves you, Jordan."

"We love you too," said Jade. "How's it going down there?"

"Pretty good," replied Connor. "I kinda like it down here, Jade. There's so much to do, and the houses are huge. I'll have to bring you down here one weekend and show you around."

"Sounds good to me. I miss you so much, Connor."

"I miss you too," said Connor. "I'll see you tomorrow, love. Good night."

"Oh Connor, try to get back early because we have a meeting with Ava Saturday morning."

"I will," said Connor.

"Okay. Good night," said Jade.

By the time Jade got off the phone with Connor, Jordan was asleep. *Great*, thought Jade, *I can get some sleep now.* Twenty minutes later, Jordan woke up again.

"No, Jordan," cried Jade. "You gotta sleep." Mommy's tired.

Jade wondered if Sophia or Becca were available to come over and stay with Jordan for a while. Jade texted Sophia and Becca and patiently waited for a response. Ten, twenty, thirty minutes passed; no response from Sophia or Becca.

Jade thought about texting Nelson but she hadn't seen Nelson since he kissed her. Jade had forgiven Nelson for the unexpected kiss, but he didn't know that. She silently prayed and sent Nelson a text.

Hey Nelson, sorry for the late text, but Jordan is still awake, and she will not let me sleep LOL. Would you mind coming over and watching her for a couple of hours.

Nelson responded right away: *I'll be right over.*

Jade put on a tank top and a pair of Connor's basketball shorts. Then she sat on the bed and cradled Jordan in her arms. Twenty minutes later, she heard the doorbell. *He must have sped all the way here*, she thought.

"There she is," said Nelson.

Jade handed Jordan to Nelson and locked the door.

"Thanks so much, Nelson," said Jade.

"No worries," said Nelson. "Class went a little late tonight, and I was on my way home anyway."

"Oh wow," said Jade. "You had class tonight? It was selfish of me to bother you, Nelson. I apologize."

"You're not a bother. Any chance I can get to see this little beauty is fine with me," said Nelson.

"Thanks so much," said Jade.

"She's growing," said Nelson as he kissed Jordan on her cheek.

"Yes, she is," said Jade. Jade turned on the light and sat down. "I just wish she would sleep."

"I know you're tired, but I was hoping you had a few minutes to talk," said Nelson.

"Of course. What's up?"

Nelson lounged back on the couch. He rubbed Jordan's back as she rested on his chest.

"I need to tell you something," said Nelson. "Connor is like a brother to me, and I would never do anything to hurt him, but ever since I saw you at Club Paradise, I have thought about being with you."

"Club Paradise? That was almost two years ago, Nelson."

"I know, but to me, it seems like yesterday. I remember seeing you at the bar, looking sexy in that gold top."

"You remember what I was wearing?"

"Sure do," replied Nelson. "You were glowing. Some dude was talking to you, and he made you smile. And when I saw you smile, something inside me warmed right up. I looked for you in the club, and when I found you, you were dancing with Connor. And the way you two were looking at each other...I just knew. That night, Connor talked about you all the way home. I knew then that he was serious about you, and there was no way I was going to interfere, so I stepped off. I just want you to know that I care about you, Jade, I really do."

"So that's what that kiss was about?"

"Yes," replied Nelson. "I think you're amazing, Jade. You're beautiful, and you love with your whole heart. I pray that I find someone like you one day."

"I'm sure you will, Nelson. Thanks for the compliment and for sharing your feelings with me."

Jade's eyes began to water.

"What's wrong?" Nelson asked.

"Connor *is* my life, Nelson, and I love him completely."

"I know," said Nelson as he stared into Jade's eyes. "And I..."

"There's more?"

"Yes. I'm moving to Miami after the wedding," replied Nelson.

"Miami! Does Connor know?"

"Not yet," replied Nelson. "I'll tell him after the wedding."

"We're going to miss you, Nelson."

"I'm going to miss y'all too," said Nelson. "Go get some sleep. Jordan and I will be fine out here."

Jade turned off the light and headed to the bedroom. She stopped midway, turned around, and walked over to the couch. She leaned down and gave Jordan a kiss. Then she looked at Nelson. The darkness lifted just enough for Jade to see that his eyes were closed. She smiled and kissed Nelson on his lips. Nelson opened his eyes and looked at Jade.

"Thank you, Jade," he whispered.

"Thank you, Nelson."

22

Connor looked forward to getting home and seeing his girls, but when he returned from his trip, he felt a bit uneasy. His thoughts ran rampant, and he couldn't sleep. When Connor woke up Saturday morning, he felt drained and needed something to stimulate his veins. On the way to Ava's office, Connor and Jade stopped at McDonald's for coffee.

Ava smiled at Jade and Connor as they entered her office. She was excited to see them, and anxious to finalize the wedding details.

"Well, hello," said Ava.

"Hi, Ava," said Jade. "Thanks for seeing us on a Saturday."

"No problem. I reserve Saturdays for my busy clients."

"We appreciate it," said Connor.

"Oh my, look at this beauty," said Ava. "She's adorable."

"Thanks," said Connor.

"Have a seat," said Ava. "So, we are getting close to the wedding. Are you guys excited?"

"Absolutely," replied Jade. "We can't wait. I pick up my dress in two weeks."

"Great! Which wedding cake did you decide on?" Ava asked.

"We like the three-tiered cake decorated in our wedding colors," replied Jade.

"Great choice," said Ava.

Jade and Connor looked at each other and smiled. Connor grabbed Jade's hand, raised it to his lips, and kissed it.

"And the songs. What have you two lovebirds come up with as Jade walks down the aisle?"

"Well, we went way back to a song my mom loves," replied Jade as she smiled and looked at Connor. "We listened to it a few times, and we agree that it's fitting for our special day."

"What song is that?" Ava asked.

"'Spend My Life with You' by Eric Benet," replied Connor. "And for our first dance song we chose 'You and I' by Avant."

"Nice. And what about the father-daughter song?" Ava asked.

"I apologize. I haven't talked to my dad about that yet," replied Jade.

"Okay," said Ava. "Please text me the title as soon as you can. I need to finish putting your package together."

"I will," said Jade.

"Now what about the juice fountain?" Ava asked.

"We were hoping you could just choose one for us since you're the pro." Connor laughed. "We'll be fine with whatever you decide."

"Okay. I'll take care of that today."

"Wonderful! You guys are all set. I'll be in Georgia three days before the wedding to make sure everything is on track. If I run into any SNAFUs I'll let you know."

"Thank you very much," said Connor. "You have been great."

"Thanks, but we're not done yet."

"I know," said Connor. "Our parents still have to pay you." He laughed.

"They're definitely taking care of that, so don't you worry," said Ava.

"Okay. Have a great day," said Jade as she and Connor left Ava's office.

When Connor and Jade got home, Jade warmed up a bottle of milk and fed Jordan. After Jordan's feeding, Connor took his girls to the park. He took family selfies with Jade and Jordan and then recorded Jade as she slid down the slide with Jordan in her arms.

After the park, Jade and Connor went home and had an afternoon snack. As they ate, Jade attempted to strike up a conversation with Connor, but Connor didn't seem interested in talking. Connor's short responses and silence were beginning to bother Jade.

"Are you okay?" Jade asked.

"Yeah. Why?"

"Well, you didn't say much last night, and you haven't said much today," said Jade.

"How come you haven't decided on a father-daughter song yet?"

"It hasn't really been on my mind, Connor."

"Do you want to get married, Jade?"

"Of course, I do," replied Jade. "I've just been busy with Jordan, and it kept slipping my mind. I'll call my dad after dinner, okay?"

"Okay," said Connor. "I'm gonna run out for a minute. You need anything?"

"Nope," replied Jade.

Connor kissed Jade and walked out the door. He got in his BMW and sent Nelson a text: *Meet me at AJ Gators in 20.*

Twenty-five minutes later, Connor rolled up in front of AJ Gators. He parked his car and went inside the restaurant.

"Hey, man, what's up?" Connor asked.

"What's up with you?"

"I had to get out of the house," replied Connor.

"Everything okay?" Nelson asked.

"I need a drink," replied Connor.

"Hey Silas," yelled Nelson. "Get my boy here a rum and coke."

"Coming right up," yelled Silas.

Connor stared at his drink. His thoughts were heavy, and he needed to vent.

"C, man, I can tell something is on your mind. Just let it out."

"Can we get out of here?"

"What! You just got here."

"I know, but I'd rather talk at your place."

"Wait, hold up," said Nelson. "I just spotted two cuties at the end of the bar. Let me send them a drink."

"Are you serious!"

"Chill man," said Nelson. "It'll only take a sec."

"Silas, send those two ladies a shot of whatever it is they're drinking," said Nelson.

"Sure thing," said Silas.

Silas did as Nelson asked. The ladies smiled at Nelson and raised their shot glasses to thank him.

"Are you ready now?" Connor asked

"Yeah, let's go." Nelson waved goodbye to the ladies. He wanted to stay and get acquainted, but Connor needed him, and Nelson wanted to be there for his best friend.

When Connor and Nelson arrived at his apartment, he noticed the disturbed look on Connor's face.

"Lisa still threatening you, isn't she?"

"Yeah," replied Connor.

"Why don't you go to the police?"

"Nah, man," replied Connor. "I got something for her ass if I see her. Lisa is the least of my worries right now. Something else is bothering me."

"What is it?"

"Jade hasn't even decided on a father-daughter song yet. We're getting married in a few weeks. Why is she procrastinating?"

"Bro, you can't be serious," said Nelson. "You're sweating over a damn song. What's really bothering you?"

"Damn, bro. You're really gonna be one hell of a doctor," said Connor.

"So are you gonna tell me what's up, or what?" said Nelson.

"I think Jade is seeing someone," replied Connor.

"What? No way, bro!"

"Jade seemed different when I got home yesterday," said Connor. "Like she had something to tell me but didn't know how."

Nelson's facial expression changed. He felt anxious and needed to relax. Nelson stood up and walked toward the window.

"What are you talking about, C?"

"Nelson, I smelled a man's cologne on my couch, and it wasn't anything I wear. Some guy was at my house," shouted Connor. "If she's cheating on me, I swear man, it will kill me."

Nelson had a flashback. *Why didn't Jade tell Connor I was there? There was nothing to hide*, thought Nelson.

"C, Jade is not cheating on you. She loves you, bro."

"I know, and I feel that she does, I really do, but the thought of her cheating bothered me so much that I couldn't make love to her last night."

"How did you get out of that one?"

"I told her I was too tired from the trip," replied Connor. "But she knew I was bullshitting. She's not stupid."

"Now that is the one truth you said today," said Nelson.

Nelson walked to the fridge and grabbed two beers. He wrestled with the thought of telling Connor that it was his cologne he smelled, but it was too late to come clean now. The damage was done. Connor would be livid if he found out that Nelson was at his house, expressing his feelings to Jade and stealing kisses that were undoubtedly meant for him. Nelson's actions were unforgiveable, and he knew it. He had made up his mind. Connor could never know that he was there.

"Here you go, C. And I can assure you man, Jade isn't cheating on you. Now stop worrying and let's talk about your bachelor party."

"Good idea," said Connor. "Call Marcus."

Nelson called Marcus and put him on speaker. They talked about a few ideas for Connor's bachelor party. After thirty minutes of the conversation going in circles, Connor and his friends decided that they would rather hang out at Club Paradise with their friends.

23

Jade was overly excited because today was her final fitting, and she was bringing her wedding dress home. Connor laughed as Jade kept peeping out the window, checking to see if her mother had arrived.

"Relax. She'll be here soon," said Connor.

"Let me check one more time," said Jade.

Jade looked out the window again and yelled, "She's here."

"Okay, baby. Y'all have fun," said Connor.

"We will. Jordan's bottles are in the fridge. She'll be hungry when she wakes up."

"I got it, boo. Tell your mom I said hello."

"I will," said Jade.

Jade gave Connor a kiss, grabbed her purse off the chair, and ran downstairs to meet her mother.

"Hey, Ma," shouted Jade as she jumped in the car and gave her mother a kiss.

"Hey, sweetie. How is my grandbaby doing?"

"Wonderful," replied Jade. "She's growing every day, and yet she's still so small."

"I know, sweetie. You and your brother grew quick. One day y'all were babies, then y'all were graduating high school."

Jade laughed and smiled at her mother.

"I can't wait to see the dress on me again. The shop made the final alterations last week, so today we will see how they look."

"I'm still in awe at how good you look, baby. That trainer did a great job in a short period of time."

"Thanks," said Jade.

"I'm so happy for you and Connor," said her mother. "He's a great young man, Jade."

"I know," said Jade.

When Jade and her mother arrived at Wedding Bliss, they hurried out of the car and went inside the store. Once inside, Jade noticed the store was a bit crowded and hoped she wouldn't have to wait too long for Monique.

"Welcome to Wedding Bliss," said a young lady. "May I help you?"

"Yes," replied Jade. "I have an appointment with Monique. Is she here?"

"She is," replied the young lady. "Let me get her for you. Have a seat."

"So how's Dad? Still trying to get in shape for my wedding."

"He sure is, and he's doing great," replied her mother. "He's eating better, and exercising more, and he lost weight. Wait till you see him."

"Send me a pic, please," begged Jade. "So guess what song daddy chose for our dance?"

"What?"

"'You're A Big Girl Now' by the Stylistics," said Jade.

"That's a great song," said her mother.

"Ava thought so too," said Jade. "Oh good, here comes Monique."

Monique appeared from the rear of the store. She walked over to Jade and introduced herself to Jade's mother.

"Hi there. You must be Jade's mom," said Monique. "How are you?"

"Fine," replied Tanya. "Yes, I am. And how are you?"

"Just dandy," replied Monique. "It has been so much fun work-ing with Jade and her bridesmaids. Come with me, ladies. Time to try on your beautiful wedding dress."

Jade and her mother followed Monique to one of the dressing areas in the rear of the store.

"Have a seat," said Monique. "I'll be right back." Jade and her mother sat down on the plush sofa couch while Monique went to get Jade's dress.

"All righty," said Monique. "Here we are. Jade, go change into a slip so we can get this gorgeous dress on you."

Jade ran inside the dressing room and put on the dress slip that awaited her. After Jade put on the dress slip, she stepped out of the dressing room and Monique helped her put on her wedding dress.

"Beautiful, just beautiful," said Monique.

"Baby, you look stunning!"

"Thanks, Mom. You really like it?"

"Absolutely," replied her mother.

"Perfect fit," said Monique as she smiled at Jade. "Would you like to take a few pictures of your daughter in her wedding dress?"

"Oh, yes," replied Tanya.

Jade posed while her mother took a few pictures of her. When they were done, Monique helped Jade out of the dress.

"Once I wrap the dress, you ladies will be all set."

"Thank you, Monique," said Jade. "I'll send you pictures."

"That would be great," said Monique. "I'll put them on our website."

"Would you really?" Jade asked.

"Sure will," replied Monique.

Monique took the dress and left the dressing area. When she returned, she had Jade's dress in her arms, all wrapped up in a Wedding Bliss garment bag.

"Here you go, Jade," said Monique.

"Thanks again, Monique."

"My pleasure," said Monique. "Enjoy the rest of your day, ladies."

"You too," said Jade.

Jade and her mother left the store and headed home. On the way home, Jade's stomach growled. She looked at her mother and laughed.

"Sounds like you're hungry, sweetheart. So what's good to eat in your neck of the woods?"

"Everything," replied Jade. "I love the food at Vinny's though. Wanna go?"

"That's fine with me," her mother replied.

Jade gave her mother directions to Vinny's. When they entered the restaurant, they walked toward a booth near the register and sat down. Jade saw Renz and waved hello. A short girl with purple highlights in her hair met Jade and her mother at the table. She put two cups of water on the table and then she handed Jade and her mother a menu. A few seconds later, Renz walked over to their table with a smile on his face.

"How you doing, Jade?" Renz asked.

"Great," replied Jade. "How have you been?"

"Rather good," replied Renz. "Long time no see."

"I know," said Jade. "I've been quite busy."

"So did I miss the wedding or what?"

"No, you haven't." Jade laughed. "The wedding is July first."

"Wow, that's right around the corner," said Renz.

"It sure is, and I'm so excited," said Jade.

"You're going to be a beautiful bride," said Renz as he stared at Jade.

Tanya cleared her throat and looked at Jade.

"Oh, my bad," said Jade. "Renz, this is my mom. Mom, this is my friend, Renz."

"Nice to meet you, ma'am," said Renz.

"Same here," said Tanya.

"So did you have a boy or a girl?" Renz asked with admiration.

"I had a girl," replied Jade. "You want to see her?"

"Sure," replied Renz.

Renz sat down next to Jade. Jade pulled her phone out and showed Renz a few pictures of her daughter.

"We named her Jordan Marie."

"She's beautiful," said Renz.

"Thank you," said Jade.

"Ladies, take your time and let me know when y'all are ready to order."

"Okay. Thank you," said Tanya.

Renz got up from the table and went back to work. Jade and her mother looked over the menu for a few minutes.

"Jade, baby?"

"Yes, Mom."

"Is there something going on between you and Nelson?"

"What do you mean?"

"Baby, I saw the way Nelson looked at you when he stopped by the house. And at Jordan's christening, he couldn't keep his eyes off you. I know love when I see it, and that boy loves you."

"Mom, Nelson cares about me, that's it! He *is* Jordan's godfather, you know."

"Jade, you're a smart girl, and I know you're not that naive. So believe me when I say, Nelson loves you. What I want to know is, do you have feelings for him?"

"For God's sake, Mom. Connor and I are getting married in a few weeks," replied Jade. "Nelson"—Jade hesitated—"is the farthest thing from my mind, and no, I do not have feelings for him."

Jade was caught off guard. Of all the things her mother could have asked her, Jade was not expecting to be questioned about Nelson. Of course, she thought about Nelson. Nelson had kissed her. He had come over to watch Jordan so she could rest, and Nelson had expressed his true feelings for her.

Ever since Nelson told Jade how he felt about her, she found herself thinking about him more often. But Jade couldn't disclose her thoughts to her mother or anyone else for that matter. No one could know her private thoughts about Nelson. Nelson shared his most intimate feelings with her, and she vowed to keep his words close to her heart.

24

As Connor got dressed for his bachelor party, he blasted the music on his phone to pump himself up. Then he sprayed on Jade's favorite cologne and did a silly dance move in front of the mirror. Jade shook her head and laughed. Connor turned around, grabbed Jade's hands, and spun her around.

"Okay, baby, I'm out," said Connor. "Do I look good or what?"

"You sure do," replied Jade. "I see you're finally wearing your Father's Day gift."

"Of course," said Connor. "This herringbone chain is dope. You did good, baby."

"Don't go getting into any trouble." Jade laughed.

"Me? No way," said Connor. "All the trouble I want is right here."

"Ha, ha, ha. And why you gotta wear my favorite cologne? If I like it, don't you think some other girl will too?"

Connor laughed and said, "I'll see you later tonight. Sophie and Becca coming over?"

"Yeah. They'll be here soon," replied Jade.

"Cool. Gotta go. And please be naked when I get back," said Connor.

"Boy, get outta here." Jade laughed.

Connor grabbed his linen blazer off the couch, checked his back pockets to make sure he had his wallet, and headed to the garage. He looked ravishingly handsome in his sky-blue linen outfit. Connor jumped into his BMW and took one last look at himself in the rear-view mirror.

"You're one fine looking dude," he said.

When Connor arrived at Nelson's house, he let himself in and rushed to the kitchen to get a beer.

"You ready?" Connor asked anxiously.

"Yeah. I'm coming," replied Nelson. "Marcus and the crew will meet us there."

"Good, because I'm ready to get my groove on," yelled Connor.

"Okay, let's go," said Nelson.

"Hold up. Let me take a quick piss," said Connor.

Connor went to use the bathroom. He washed his hands and looked at himself in the mirror. As Connor dried his hands, he saw a bottle of cologne sitting on the shelf.

"He got some new shit and didn't tell me," said Connor. Connor walked over to the shelf and opened the bottle of cologne. The strong scent hit him like a thick wave. "That's the same scent I smelled on my couch," whispered Connor. "What the fuck!"

Connor rushed out of the bathroom. He was fired up. *No way could that have been Nelson on my couch. Nelson is my boy. He's like a brother to me*, thought Connor. *Why was he at my house? Why didn't he tell me the truth about the cologne? Why didn't Jade tell me Nelson was at the house?* Connor felt betrayed. But Jade's betrayal hurt him to the core. Connor loved Jade with all his heart, and he was about to marry her. *This can't be happening*, thought Connor.

"Yo, Nelson," said Connor.

"Yeah, man, what's up?" Nelson asked as he turned around.

Connor responded with a punch to Nelson's face. Nelson stumbled back and fell into the chair. He touched the side of his face and felt a wet substance. He knew it was blood.

"That's what's up, motherfucker," yelled Connor. "It was you, wasn't it? Why were you at my house?"

"C, man, let me explain," replied Nelson.

"Why did you lie to me? You messing with Jade?"

"Connor, let me explain," repeated Nelson. "I went over to your house because Jade…"

"Because Jade what? You know what man, I'm out," shouted Connor. "Stay the hell away from me and my family."

Nelson wanted to explain what happened. He tried to stop Connor from leaving, but Connor was too enraged to listen. Connor swung the door open and left. Nelson went to the bathroom and cleaned himself up. He thought about what transpired and felt bad for hurting Connor.

Nelson realized he should have told Connor about the cologne. But Nelson had other worries. How could he tell Connor about the cologne without telling him how he felt about Jade. Nelson knew Connor would have asked probing questions that he wasn't ready to answer.

Nelson sat on the couch for a few minutes, trying to figure out what to do. He felt ashamed for hurting Connor, and at the same time, he felt the need to protect Jade. In the eight years that Nelson had known Connor, he had never seen Connor get upset, and he worried what Connor would do when he got home. Despite Connor's anger, Nelson was more than certain that Connor and Jade belonged together, and he was determined to make things right. Nelson grabbed his car keys and ran out the door.

* * *

Connor got in his car and drove around aimlessly for a while. He needed to cool off before he got home and confronted Jade about Nelson. When Connor stopped at a traffic light, he sent Jade a text: *I'm heading home. We gotta talk.*

Connor was agitated and needed another beer. He parked down the street from the corner store, jumped out of his car, and went into the store. He nodded hello to the cashier and made his way to the beer section. Connor grabbed two cans of beer and headed to the register.

As Connor walked out of the store, he saw a young man lean-ing against the building. Connor and the young man looked at each other for a second before Connor continued to his car.

"Hey, are you Connor?" the young man asked.

"Yeah. Who the fuck wants to know?" Connor asked. Connor turned around to face the young man.

The young man pulled out a gun, pointed it at Connor, and pulled the trigger.

"That's for hurting my sister, asshole."

Connor's body fell to the ground. The bag he was holding fell from his hand, and the beer cans rolled out of the bag and down the street. The young man leaned over Connor's body and ripped the diamond earring out of his ear.

"You won't be needing this anymore," he whispered.

The cashier heard the gunshot and called the police. He ran out of the store and saw someone dressed in all black run away and disappear into the darkness.

The cashier walked farther down the street. His eyes were imme-diately met with a body lying on the ground. The body was still. The cashier leaned over the body and noticed the gunshot wound to Connor's head. Within minutes, a few people gathered around the scene.

A lady in the crowd cried, "Oh, my god."

Another lady voiced quietly to her friend, "Let's get outta here before the police come."

The crowd got larger as people ran toward the scene from all directions.

A few minutes later, two cop cars arrived at the scene. The detec-tives arrived ten minutes later, followed by the crime scene investiga-tors, and finally the paramedics.

The policemen made their way through the crowd and attempted to get things under control.

"Okay, people, please move away from the area," yelled the offi-cer. "This is an active crime scene. Please move back."

Two officers moved the crowd away from the area while the other two officers placed yellow tape around the crime scene. Detectives Steiner and Fraiser observed the crowd for any relevant clues.

A few seconds later, the cashier walked up to the detectives.

"Are you the one who called this in?" Detective Steiner asked.

"Yes," replied the cashier.

"I'm Detective Steiner. Let's go inside and talk. I'm going to need a full statement from you."

"No problem," said the cashier.

"Fraiser, make sure these people stay out of the way."

"I'm on it, Steiner."

The crime scene investigators got to work taking pictures and collecting evidence from the scene. A female investigator checked Connor's pockets and pulled out a wallet, car keys, and a cell phone. She then noticed the gold chain around Connor's neck and removed it. The investigator put the items in a bag and handed the bag to Detective Fraiser.

When Detective Steiner exited the store, he and Detective Fraiser got in the car and headed to the address on the driver's license.

"So who's our John Doe?" Steiner asked.

"One Conario Ellis," replied Fraiser. "Twenty-four years old. Address is two-fourteen Ivory Court, apartment two alpha."

"Damn, I hate this part of the job," said Steiner. "Guess we better go notify his family."

* * *

Nelson parked his car across the street from Jade's apartment. He looked up toward the balcony and noticed the lights were on. Nelson ran inside the building and leaped up the stairs. He heard music and laughter coming from Jade's apartment. Nelson rang the doorbell repeatedly. Finally, Jade answered.

"Hey, Nelson," said Jade as she opened the door. "What are you doing here?"

"Can I come in?" Nelson asked as he tried to catch his breath.

"Of course," replied Jade.

Jade noticed Nelson's bruised face and bloody shirt as he stepped inside the apartment.

"What the hell happened to you, and where is Connor?" Jade asked in a panic.

"Jade, please calm down," replied Nelson. "We need to talk."

Nelson followed Jade into the living room. Jade rushed to the kitchen and grabbed a small bag of frozen vegetables for his face. Sophia and Becca heard the commotion and went to see what was going on.

"Whoa!" Sophia yelled. "What the hell happened to you?"

"Sophie, move back," said Jade. "Here, Nelson, put this on your eye."

"Thanks, Jade."

"Are you okay?" Becca asked.

"I'm fine," replied Nelson. "Jade, I gotta talk to you, now."

"Sorry, ladies, but I gotta call it a night. I'll call y'all tomorrow."

Sophie and Becca grabbed their things and left. Jade sat down next to Nelson and began to worry. The only thing on her mind was Connor, and she hoped that he was okay.

Jade looked at Nelson with much concern, and asked, "Where's Connor?"

"He's not here yet?"

"No," replied Jade. "And why would he be, Nelson? Y'all are supposed to be at his bachelor party."

"We never made it," said Nelson. "Did Connor call you?"

"What do you mean, you never made it?"

"Where's your phone?" Nelson asked.

Jade grabbed her phone off the table and realized that Connor had sent her a text.

"Connor texted me forty minutes ago," said Jade.

"What did he say?"

"That he's heading home and wants to talk," replied Jade.

"Damn, he should've been here by now," said Nelson.

"I better call him," said Jade.

Jade called Connor and got his voicemail. She left him a message and turned her attention to Nelson.

"Now what the hell is going on, Nelson?"

Nelson leaned back and told Jade what happened. Through the throbbing pain and anxiety, he was able to get a few words out.

"Connor hit the roof when he found out that I was here that night," said Nelson.

"But why would Connor get upset over that?" Jade asked.

"Because neither one of us told him," replied Nelson. "So Connor assumed that you were cheating on him."

"What!" Jade yelled. "Why would he—"

"He smelled my cologne," replied Nelson.

"Your cologne? I'm confused," said Jade.

"My cologne, Jade. When Connor got home from his trip, he smelled my cologne on your couch, which naturally made him think that some dude was over here, and that you were cheating on him. When Connor told me about it, I freaked out and didn't tell him that I was here and that it was my cologne he smelled. I meant to throw the cologne out, but it slipped my mind. Then tonight, Connor saw the cologne in my bathroom and apparently sprayed it, and realized it was the same scent."

"Oh my goodness. Connor feels like we betrayed him," said Jade.

"Bingo!"

"I gotta go find him," cried Jade.

"Jade, stay here and wait for Connor. I'll go. I need to explain everything to him. I owe him that much."

"Oh my god, what have I done," cried Jade.

"No, Jade. What have we done? Before Connor left my place, he told me to stay away from you and Jordan. So please let me fix this. I'll bring Connor home."

As Jade walked Nelson to the door, the doorbell rang. When Jade opened the door, two detectives were standing in the doorway.

"Can I help you?" Jade asked.

"Yes, ma'am," replied the detective. "I'm Detective Steiner, and this is Detective Fraiser."

"Please come in," said Jade.

The detectives entered the apartment and followed Jade and Nelson into the living room. Jade offered them a seat, but they declined. The detectives stood in the living room, observing Jade and Nelson.

"Is Mrs. Ellis home?" Detective Steiner asked.

"Mrs. Ellis?" replied Jade.

"Yes, ma'am," replied Detective Steiner.

"Mrs. Ellis doesn't live here. Is there something I can help you with?"

"We need to contact Mrs. Ellis," said Detective Steiner. "Would you happen to have her number?"

"Of course. But I don't understand. Can you tell me what's going on, Detective?"

"What is your name, ma'am?" Detective Steiner asked.

"Jade, Jade Simpson. I'm Connor's fiancée," she replied as she grabbed her phone off the table.

"Ms. Simpson, I'm going to need your number as well," said the detective.

Jade scrolled through her contacts until she got to Mrs. Ellis's name. She gave the detective Mrs. Ellis's number, and then she gave the detective her number.

"Thanks, ma'am," said the detective.

"No problem," said Jade. "Is that it?"

"Not quite," said Detective Fraiser.

Detective Fraiser looked at Nelson suspiciously. He noticed the cut near Nelson's eye and the blood stain on his shirt.

"And who are you?" Detective Fraiser asked as he stepped in front of Nelson.

"I'm Nelson," he replied.

"Nelson who?" Detective Fraiser asked with an attitude.

"Parello," replied Nelson.

"What happened to your face, Mr. Parello?" Detective Fraiser asked.

Nelson didn't respond. He knew the law and that his words could be used against him in court.

Detective Fraiser knew he was dealing with a smart young man. He also knew that something happened between Connor and Nelson, and he needed to investigate.

"Did Mr. Ellis do that to your face?"

Nelson remained quiet. The detectives knew Connor hit him. They had seen Connor's bruised fist at the crime scene. The detectives observed how Jade and Nelson were acting while being questioned, and figured it was a clear case of a lover's quarrel gone wrong, very wrong.

"Detective, I gotta go find Connor," said Nelson. "So if you'll excuse me."

"Young man, the only place you're going is downtown with us," said Detective Fraiser. "We have a few questions we need to ask you."

"Why do you need to ask him questions?" Jade asked. "He didn't do anything."

"Ma'am, please," said Detective Steiner.

"Jade, I'll call you later," said Nelson. Nelson huffed and puffed under his breath as he followed the detectives out the door.

Jade locked the door and went into the living room. She sat down and read Connor's text again. "Where are you, Connor?" she whispered. Jade got on her knees and prayed that Connor was safe and that he would be home soon.

Jade made back-to-back phone calls to Connor, and each call went to his voicemail. She sent him a few texts and waited patiently for a response, but no response came.

Jade called Mrs. Ellis right away. As Jade told Connor's mother about the detectives, she began to cry helplessly on the phone. Mrs. Ellis told Jade to calm down and not to worry. "I'll call the detectives and call you back as soon as I can," she said.

Then Jade called her mother and told her mother what happened. "We'll be there as soon as we can," her mother said.

Jade called Connor again and got his voicemail. Nelson hadn't called her back yet, and when she called him, he didn't answer. Mrs. Ellis hadn't called her back either. And her best friends, Sophia and Becca, didn't answer her calls. Jade was all alone and didn't know what to do.

Jade was still awake when her parents arrived. She hugged her parents as they entered the apartment. When Jade looked at Jordan sleeping in her grandmother's arms, she began to cry.

"Go lay down, sweetheart," said her father. "I'll make you some tea."

Jade went into the family room to lay down. Tanya went to the nursery and put Jordan in her crib. Then she went into the family room to talk to Jade.

"Baby, Mrs. Ellis called me on our way here. She wanted to call you, but I told her that I would talk to you."

"Did they find Connor?" cried Jade. "Where is he? When will he be home?" Jade shouted.

Jade's parents looked at each other. There was no easy way to tell Jade the devastating news about Connor. Tanya and Louis knew that Jade wouldn't accept the fact that Connor was gone, and he wasn't coming home.

"Jade, baby. I'm sorry to tell you this, but Connor was robbed and shot last night," said her mother.

"What! What do you mean?" Jade cried.

"Here's your tea, sweetheart."

"Take me to the hospital," cried Jade. "I want to see Connor."

"Baby, Connor isn't coming home," her mother said.

Jade let out a deafening cry and fell into her mother's arms.

"No, no, no," screamed Jade as she gripped her mother's shirt. "Please tell me it's not true," she cried. "Why, Mom? Why Connor?"

Jade's mother didn't respond. There were no words to console Jade. She was completely devastated.

"We're so sorry, Jade," whispered her mother.

Jade cried for hours before she fell asleep in her mother's arms.

25

Connor's death was extremely heartbreaking for Jade. Jade became unglued, disoriented, and confused. Her heart was heavy, and she felt empty inside.

When Jade woke up Sunday afternoon, she went to the nursery to check on Jordan. Jordan looked like a little angel as she slept.

Jade kissed Jordan on her check and went back into the family room. She checked her phone, hoping to see a missed call from Connor, but there were no missed calls from Connor. All she saw were missed calls and texts from Becca and Sophia.

Jade called Connor and started to cry when she heard his voice on his voicemail. Then she called Nelson, but hung up when she heard his voicemail.

As Jade scrolled through her gallery of pictures, she smiled, sniffled, and wiped the tears from her eyes. She missed Connor terribly. She wanted to be with him, touch him, hold him, and kiss him.

"Hey, sweetheart. You want something to eat?"

"No, I'm not hungry," replied Jade.

"Sweetheart, you have to eat something," said her mother. "How about some eggs?"

"Sure," replied Jade.

"Oh, Sophia and Becca stopped by while you were sleeping. They're sorry about Connor and asked that you call them."

"Thanks, Mom. I'll call them later," said Jade. "I think I want to go home."

Jade's mother looked at her and said, "Now that is a great idea, sweetheart."

* * *

Monday morning, while Jade slept, her mother packed a suitcase for her and Jordan. Jade's parents were happy that she wanted to go home. Jade didn't need to be alone in the apartment, she needed to be with her family and her parents wanted to take care of her.

After breakfast, Tanya cleaned up the kitchen and dressed Jordan. When everyone was dressed and ready to go, Louis packed the SUV and took his family home to Southampton.

On the way home, Jade checked her phone to see if Nelson had called her back, but she didn't have any missed calls or texts from him.

Jade checked her Facebook page and noticed she had a few notifications from her friends. They expressed their deepest condolences for her loss. Jade closed her eyes, and as she thought about what happened to Connor, a tear rolled down her face.

She thought about Jordan not having a father, and the thought of that hurt. Jade knew she would have to be strong for Jordan, but was she ready? Jade wanted Connor. She desperately missed him and needed him like a fish needs water.

Jade sobbed as she thought about not feeling Connor's touch, not hearing Connor say her name, not kissing his soft lips, not feeling his fingers caress her body, not seeing Connor rock Jordan to sleep, and not feeling Connor inside her. Jade wanted all those things with Connor again, but those moments of affection would be no more, and the thought of that was unbearable.

* * *

For the entire week, all Jade did was shower, eat, sleep, and pump her breasts. Jade wanted to be alone in her old room. She didn't want to talk or see anyone. Jade put her phone on silent and grieved for Connor.

Tanya took care of Jordan. She checked on Jade periodically, but for the most part, she left Jade alone. Tanya knew how much Jade loved Connor and that she needed time alone to grieve.

Jade listened to all her messages. Her friends and coworkers called and left sincere messages expressing their condolences. Their love for her and Connor made Jade feel a little better; but no one would ever know the depths of her sorrow.

Jade took a shower, got dressed, and went downstairs.

"There goes my girl," said Jade's father.

"Hey," said Jade as she sat down. "I want to thank y'all for taking care of me and Jordan. I love y'all."

"We love you too, baby."

Jade looked at Jordan sleeping in her grandmother's arms. She looked peaceful, like an angel resting on a cloud.

"Mom, can I hold her?"

"Sure, baby. Here you go."

A tear rolled down Jade's face as she kissed Jordan on her cheek. Jade stared at Jordan and realized how she was beginning to look like Connor.

Jade held Jordan tight as she thought about Connor. She couldn't help but remember all the good times she had with him. She remembered how delighted Connor was when he first saw Jordan, and the many nights when Jordan cried for him. Those nights were special. Connor would jump out of the bed and run to Jordan's aid and rock her back to sleep. Or when Connor would put a comforter on the floor and lay down with Jordan on his chest as he watched television. Jade would miss those days forever.

Jade's thoughts were interrupted when her phone rang.

"Hi, Jade?"

"Yes. Who's this?"

"Renz," he replied. "I just heard about what happened. I'm so sorry, Jade. Listen, I gotta take care of a dilemma at home, and then I'll be over to see you, okay."

"I'm not home. I'm at my parents," said Jade.

"Oh. Okay. Well, I guess I'll stop by when you get back."

"But I don't know when that'll be. Plus, you need to be with your family."

"Yeah, but we're not too worried. My cousin up and leaves all the time."

"Wow, that's crazy," said Jade.

"Well, if you need to talk, just call, okay."

"Thanks, Renz. I really appreciate that. Talk to you later."

As Jade hung up with Renz, her phone rang again.

"Hello," said Jade.

"Hi, Jade. It's me, Nelson."

Jade went to the kitchen to talk privately. She had a few questions for Nelson.

"Nelson, what's going on?" Jade asked. "Where have you been? I…we needed you."

"There's no excuse for my actions," replied Nelson. "I'm sorry for not calling you sooner. And I'm sorry for not being there for you and Jordan. I had no idea what to say to you, and honestly, I still don't. I feel totally responsible for what happened to Connor, and I'm sorry."

"How do you think I feel?" Jade shouted. "You said you were going to call me back."

"I know, I know," replied Nelson. "And I feel terrible for how I handled the situation. That was wrong. Those damn detectives pissed me off. They questioned me for hours. They think I had something to do with Connor's death."

"They're wrong, Nelson. I know you didn't hurt Connor."

"Connor's death has been the hardest thing for me to deal with since my mother died, so I'm not sure how I'm gonna be able to deal with this. Are you home?" Nelson asked softly. "I want to come over and talk to you."

"I'm at my parents' house."

"Oh, okay."

"Can you ever forgive me, Jade?" Nelson asked.

"Of course," replied Jade. "Nelson, I know you loved Connor, and I know you're hurting. We are going to hurt for a long time."

"I know, but I just keep thinking that if I had told Connor the truth, none of this would've happened," said Nelson.

Jade felt the same way. And although she was hurting, she felt that Nelson needed a few words of encouragement.

"Nelson, please don't feel guilty about what happened. Connor wouldn't want that. I believe that Connor would want us to keep living and be happy. He was just that type of guy. I'm so glad that a piece of him is here with me. We gotta be strong for Jordan. We have to tell her how great her daddy was. And Jordan is going to need her godfather more than ever."

"You're right, Jade. Thank you. I needed to hear that."

"Connor's spirit will always be with me, Nelson, and knowing that makes me feel better," cried Jade.

"Don't cry," said Nelson.

"They're happy tears," said Jade. "I'm so grateful for the two years God gave me and Connor. The memories will last a lifetime."

"Yes, they will," said Nelson. "Oh, by the way, I'm thinking about postponing my internship. I need to be here for you and Jordan."

"Don't you dare do that, Nelson. Don't put your plans on hold for us. Great things are in store for you, and you're going to be a great doctor one day. Jordan and I will be fine."

"Are you sure?" Nelson asked.

"Yes," replied Jade.

"Okay," said Nelson. "Get some rest. I'll see you Saturday. And I promise to keep in touch."

26

What was supposed to be the happiest day of Jade's life turned out to be the saddest day of her life. It was a beautiful Saturday morning, a perfect day for a wedding, but instead, Jade and her family were preparing to attend Connor's homegoing service.

It took a lot for Jade to be there, but Jade knew God's strength would help her get through the day and the weeks to come. Celebrating Connor's life was what Jade had to do, even if it had to be done on their wedding day.

The ushers assisted Connor's family get situated and lined up in the lobby of the church. When everyone was lined up properly, the ushers opened the double doors to the church to begin the procession.

Pastor Wallace entered the church and quoted Psalm 23 as he walked down the aisle. Jade felt God's presence as soon as she entered the church. The atmosphere was warm and welcoming, and Jade felt safe to be in the Lord's house.

Mrs. Ellis cried softly as she walked down the aisle. Mr. Ellis held his wife tight as they made their way to the first pew. Nelson walked down the aisle with Connor's parents and held Julia's hand. Jade carried Jordan in her arms as she and her parents followed Connor's parents.

The choir sang a lovely song as Pastor Wallace made his way to the pulpit. When the choir finished singing, Pastor Wallace prayed, gave honor to God, and greeted the congregation.

"We are here today to celebrate the glorious life of Conario Ellis," he shouted.

His words were loud and electrifying. Pastor Wallace continued and delivered a touching eulogy to honor Connor's life.

"I have known Conario since he was a young boy. Today, with sadness and a heavy heart, we mourn a life that was tragically taken from us too soon. As we remember Conario, don't be afraid to grieve. Your sorrow represents the measure of love, happiness, and intimacy that each of you shared with him. We each have our own special memories of Connor.

"My memory goes back to when he started middle school. Connor was eleven years old, and he and his family had recently moved to Georgia. One Sunday afternoon, Connor ran up to me and said, 'Pastor Wallace, what if they don't like me?' And I said, 'What! You? My dear child, they will love you because you love Jesus.' Connor gave me a questionable look as he tried to decipher what I meant.

"A few weeks later, I asked Connor about school and the kids there, and Connor said, 'Pastor, you were right, the girls love me!'"

Joyous laughter filled the church as people nodded their heads up and down knowing that Connor would have said just that.

Pastor Wallace continued, "To Connor's family and friends, our vision of Connor is uniquely special. He was kind, giving, caring, honest, and loving. Connor's unselfish acts touched every person here today. Speak of Connor often, reach out to his parents from time to time, hold your memories of him close to your heart. In doing so, you will honor his legacy.

"In closing, I want to address Connor's parents, Julia and Gordon Ellis. Your life will never be the same without Connor. It's going to be a tough road ahead. A piece of your circle has been broken, but with time comes healing. Connor loved the Lord, and his soul is resting in heaven. And I know you both love the Lord. So when you find yourself not knowing what to do, or feeling despair and alone, remember that God loves you. He will be right there for you, ready to hold you, protect you, heal you, comfort you, and talk to you whenever you need him."

Pastor Wallace prayed for Connor's parents and then introduced his cousin Natalia.

"Next, we will hear a solo from Ms. Natalia Reid, followed by a praise dance from our praise team, and then comments from Connor's family and friends."

Natalia stood up and walked to the pulpit. She sang a beautiful version of "His Eye Is on the Sparrow," which made Mrs. Ellis cry. Jade watched Natalia as she sang, amazed at how poised she was on such a sad occasion. By the time Natalia was done singing, the whole church was crying.

The praise team performed a beautiful praise dance to "He Has His Hands on You." As Jade watched the praise dancers perform, she began to cry. Jade's mother embraced her and told her that everything was going to be fine.

After the praise dance, Connor's cousins and friends shared their feelings for him. Everyone had nice things to say about Connor, but Nelson said something very touching.

"Connor was the brother I never had," he said. "He was always…always there for me. I can go on for hours telling you how much Connor meant to me, but if I did, we would be here till next week. But to sum it up, Connor was a good person, and he cared about everyone he knew. He made me part of his family, and I will forever be his brother and love him always. Love you, bro."

"Amen," said the congregation.

As Connor's homegoing service came to an end, the ushers opened the casket and ushered the patrons out of the pews to pay their last respects to Connor. One by one, the patrons said their final goodbyes to Connor and took their seats.

Connor's family was next. Each family member followed suit and said goodbye to Connor. Some family members stood in front of the casket longer than others, crying and not wanting to say goodbye. Others kissed Connor goodbye and quickly took their seat.

When it was time for Jade and her family to say goodbye to Connor, Jade handed Jordan to Nelson, and she and her family walked to the casket together. Jade cried as she stared at Connor in the casket. She wanted Connor to open his eyes and talk to her. But most of all, Jade wanted to hear Connor say her name, just one more time.

Jade touched Connor's hand and placed a picture of her and Jordan in the casket. Then she gave Connor a final kiss goodbye.

"I will always love you, Connor Ellis," she whispered.

When it was time for the Ellises to say goodbye to their son, Gordon helped Julia stand up. He held Julia close to him as they walked to the casket. Julia cried as she stared at her son. She became weak and almost fainted. Nelson and one of the ushers rushed to her side and helped Gordon get Julia back to the pew.

Nelson sat down and handed Mrs. Ellis a tissue. Jade looked at Nelson as he sat stoically and maintained his composure. The only sign of grief was Nelson's hand shaking on his leg. Jade noticed and placed her hand on top of his hand and held it tight. Nelson looked at Jade, and a tear rolled down his face.

As the choir stood up to sing the final selection, Nelson and the other pallbearers assumed duty and took their assigned spots at Connor's casket. Connor's family and friends cried as the casket passed their pews. After the final selection, Pastor Wallace stepped to the pulpit, prayed for Connor's family, and gave the benediction.

* * *

Two weeks after Connor's funeral, Jade was still sad. Her only bit of happiness was when Jordan returned home from her grandparent's house in Georgia. Jade was overjoyed to see Jordan, but she also wanted to be alone. Jade dodged calls from her friends and stayed in the house. She thought about Nelson and wondered what he was doing. Nelson hadn't called her, and she hadn't called him.

There was one call that Jade did answer. Detective Steiner called and told Jade that he needed to talk to her as soon as possible. Jade informed the detective that she was staying with her parents and not sure when she would be home.

"I can come there," he told her. "Just let me know when you're available."

Jade told the detective that Monday morning would be fine.

* * *

Jade woke up early Monday morning. She fed Jordan, got dressed, and waited patiently for Detective Steiner to arrive. She made a pot of coffee just in case the detective was a coffee drinker.

When the doorbell rang, her mother answered the door and led Detective Steiner to the dining room where Jade was waiting for him. Jade stood up and shook the detective's hand.

"Good morning, Detective Steiner," said Jade.

"Good morning, Ms. Simpson. How are you doing?"

"Okay," replied Jade. "Would you like some coffee?"

"No, thank you," he replied. "Before we get started, I just want to say that I'm sorry for your loss. I understand that your wedding was planned for July first."

"Yes, it was," said Jade.

"I'm very sorry."

"Thank you," said Jade.

"I just have a few questions for you. We need to clear up a few things to rule out persons of interest."

"I understand," said Jade.

"I have to ask…but we need to know what type of relationship do you have with Mr. Parello?"

"Nelson!" Jade replied.

"Yes," replied Detective Steiner. "Were the two of you seeing each other?"

"No!" yelled Jade. "Nelson and I are friends. He's Jordan's godfather."

"Who is Jordan?"

"My daughter," replied Jade.

"Oh, I see," said the detective.

Jade watched the detective write something down in his green hand-sized notepad.

"So you and Mr. Parello weren't having an affair?"

"How dare you imply that something was going on between me and Nelson," shouted Jade. "I love Connor, and I do not appreciate you coming to my parents' house, accusing us of having an affair."

"Ms. Simpson, I'm not accusing you of anything," said the detective. "My job is to fact-check and verify all angles. I have seen too many situations like this in my years, and my job is to do a thorough investigation."

"Have you talked to Mr. Parello lately?"

"I haven't talked to Nelson since the funeral. Why? Is Nelson a suspect?"

"No, ma'am," replied Detective Steiner. "It turns out that Mr. Parello said the same thing you said. I needed to hear what you had to say before we cleared him."

"Nelson would never hurt Connor," said Jade. "They were like brothers."

"We are beginning to realize that, ma'am. But like I said, we see a lot of situations like this, and we had to be sure that Mr. Parello had nothing to do with Connor's death. I need to ask you one more question."

Jade sat quietly and waited for the detective's question. She sipped her coffee and crossed her arms. When Jade looked at the detective, he was flipping pages in his notepad.

"Do you know a Lisa Flores?"

"No, sir," replied Jade.

"Are you sure, ma'am?"

"Yes," replied Jade. "Why?"

"Because prior to Connor's death, she sent him some pretty intense texts."

"What!" yelled Jade. "What are you talking about?"

"Do you think that Lisa and Connor may have been seeing each other?"

"No way," replied Jade. "Connor wasn't seeing any Lisa Flora, or whatever her name is."

"How can you be so sure?" Detective Steiner asked. "We know they worked together, and apparently Lisa was fired a few weeks before Connor's death."

"I wouldn't know if she was fired or not," said Jade. "You might want to talk to Connor's uncle about that."

"Oh, we got that covered, ma'am."

"Did you say Lisa?" Jade asked curiously.

"Yes," replied the detective.

"Now that I think of it, Connor received a call from a girl named Lisa last May," said Jade. "And later that night, she called Connor again. Connor said that she was a new girl in the office, and the call was about work."

"Anything else you remember, ma'am?"

"No sir," replied Jade.

"Do you recall if Connor's mood or attitude changed in the last few months?"

"Well, I'm not sure if this is important, but the day before my baby shower, Connor came home from work annoyed about something. Something was bothering him, but he didn't want to talk about it, and I didn't pry. When Connor woke up the next day, he seemed fine, and that was it."

The detective nodded his head and wrote something in his notepad again.

"Thank you for your time, Ms. Simpson. You have been very helpful."

"You're welcome, Detective. Can I ask you a question?"

"Sure," replied Detective Steiner.

"When will I get Connor's things?"

"Ma'am?"

"His wallet, his chain, his cell, and his earring."

"Those items stay in our custody until the case is closed."

Jade stared at the detective with a blank look on her face.

"Are you going to be okay? You look a bit flushed."

"Yes, I'll be fine," replied Jade as she leisurely waved her hand to dismiss the detective's concern.

"Okay. I'll be on my way then," said the detective. "Thanks again for taking the time to speak to me."

"You're welcome," said Jade.

Jade walked Detective Steiner to the door and let him out. She pulled her phone out of her pocket and called Nelson. If anyone knew if Connor was messing around with Lisa, Nelson would. After the fourth ring, Jade heard Nelson's voicemail and hung up.

27

By the end of July, Jade was still a mess. She thought about Connor every day. She thought about their apartment and how hard it was going to be for her to stay there alone. Jade didn't want to sleep alone or wake up in an empty bed. She didn't want to see Connor's clothes in the closet, and she didn't want to see Connor's pictures staring at her. That would be unbearable, and Jade wasn't ready for that.

One night, during dinner with her family, Jade asked her parents if she and Jordan could stay with them for a while.

"I just need a little time to regroup and figure things out," she told them.

Jade's parents didn't answer or object. Her father got up from the table and called U-Haul.

"I'll call Julia and let her know," said her mother.

"Thanks, Mom."

"And what are you going to do about your job?" her mother asked.

"Not sure," replied Jade. "Naomi said I can take as much time as I need, but honestly, I don't want to go back to work. I want to be here with Jordan."

"I think that is a great idea, sweetie."

"Okay, ladies. The truck is reserved for next Saturday. I'll call Justin and Zaria and ask them to help us."

"Thanks, Dad," said Jade. "I really appreciate everything you guys are doing for me."

"Jade, we love you," said her mother. "There's nothing we wouldn't do for you or Justin."

"I know, but I feel like a burden."

"You're not a burden," said her father. "You're a blessing. You and Justin. Don't ever feel like you're bothering us or altering our lives. We chose to have kids, and it is our job to take care of you and your brother."

"Thanks, Dad."

After dinner, Jade sent Renz a text to let him know she would be in town. Renz replied right away. *Hyd Jade. I'll be out of town then. Sorry that I won't get to see you. I do hope all is well. Renz.*

* * *

When Jade opened the door to her apartment, it felt lifeless. The apartment was cold and dark. Jade immediately turned up the thermostat. She put Jordan in her crib and covered her with two blankets to keep her warm.

Jade returned to the family room and opened the curtains to let the sun in. As Jade looked around the room, she saw the lovely pictures of her and Connor. Jade smiled and touched the pictures with her fingers. When Jade reached the mantel, she saw a card with her name on it, leaning against a picture of Jordan. Jade sat down and read the card.

> *Dear Jade, I hope you're doing well. I just want you to know that Connor adored you. The day after he met you, he called me and told me that he had met the girl that he was going to marry. I know in my heart that you and Connor loved each other. You made my son very happy, and I thank you for that. Healing will come with time, Jade. I want you*

to keep smiling, be happy, and continue to love. And know that we are here for you if you ever need us. Love always, Julia and Gordon Ellis.

Jade wiped her tears away and put the card in her backpack.

"Okay, y'all, let's get to work," she said.

Jade and her family got to work packing her things. Jade's mother cleaned out the fridge and made sure the dishwasher was empty.

Her father and Justin headed to the nursery to breakdown Jordan's furniture. Jade and Zaria went to her room to pack her clothes. Zaria emptied the contents of the drawers, and Jade started on the closet.

All of Connor's clothes were gone. The only item hanging on his side of the closet was Jade's wedding dress. Jade fell to her knees and started to cry.

"Oh, Jade, I'm so sorry. I should have moved your dress," said Zaria as she sat down beside her.

"No, no," cried Jade. "It's okay, Zaria. I just wish Connor had seen me in my dress."

"Me too," said Zaria. "Let me help you up."

"Where should I put your dress?" Zaria asked.

"Throw it in my suitcase," replied Jade.

"Okay," said Zaria. "When did Connor's parents clean out his things?"

"I have no idea," replied Jade.

Jade gathered the rest of her clothes and shoes and threw them in the suitcase. When Jade and Zaria were done packing her clothes, they went to the nursery to pack Jordan's clothes.

"Jordan has the cutest little outfits," said Zaria.

"Doesn't she," said Jade. "And when are you and Justin going to have a baby?"

"I hope soon," replied Zaria. "We are trying."

"In God's time," said Jade.

"Amen to that," said Zaria.

"Now this is a nice picture of Nelson and Jordan," said Zaria.

"It is, isn't it?" said Jade as she walked over to Zaria. "I really like that picture. Nelson looked so handsome that day."

"This was at Jordan's christening, right?"

"Yeah," replied Jade.

"How's Nelson doing anyway?"

"I wish I knew," replied Jade. "I get his voicemail every time I call him. And he hasn't returned my calls or responded to any of my texts. And he promised that he would keep in touch…so much for that."

"He's probably taking Connor's death harder than you think, Jade. Continue to reach out to him. He'll come around."

"I'm praying he does," said Jade.

"He will," said Zaria. "He seems like a really cool dude."

"He is, but when I see him, I'm gonna kick his ass for not keeping in touch like he promised," said Jade.

Jade and her family packed everything, including the pictures of her and Connor.

28

In August, Jade celebrated her birthday at home with her family. She longed for a birthday kiss from Connor that would never come.

Jade's friends called to wish her happy birthday. But Nelson didn't call; he sent her a text wishing her happy birthday. He didn't even ask her how she and Jordan were doing, nothing, just a happy birthday text. Nelson's actions or lack thereof hurt Jade. Nelson broke his promise again, and Jade was upset.

Mrs. Ellis called Jade to say happy birthday and told her that she and Gordon were going home to Italy to spend time with her family.

In September, Jade made up her mind and decided not to go back to work. She called Naomi and submitted her resignation. Naomi was sad that she was losing a valuable employee, but she understood.

Jade had good days and bad days. She savored every good day she spent with Jordan and her family. The bad days creeped up on her like a thief in the night. One moment Jade would be happy, and then she would hear or see something on television that reminded her of Connor. Those were her bad days.

Nelson finally called and apologized for not keeping in touch like he had promised. Jade forgave Nelson, but not before she gave him a piece of her mind. Nelson told Jade about his internship and about the interesting things he was learning. Nelson shared stories about Miami with Jade in hopes to uplift her spirits. He sent Jade pictures of him hanging out with his fellow interns and pictures of Miami's spectacular sunsets and beautiful beaches.

Nelson ended the call with an invitation for Jade to visit him in Miami. Nelson wanted to take Jade to the beach and share the sunsets with her. He wanted to treat Jade to a lovely dinner at Havana 1957, and then top the night off at a Miami Heat game. *"I'll take care of your plane ticket, just come visit me and have some fun,"* he said. But Jade declined his invitation.

The few times when Jade called Nelson, she told him how much Jordan was growing and looking more like Connor, and how Jordan would make the cutest baby faces when she tried to talk, and that one little baby tooth was starting to grow.

Nelson enjoyed the video chats the most. He loved seeing Jordan's face and her smile. *"Let me see my goddaughter,"* he'd say, and Jade would turn her phone toward Jordan. *"She's beautiful,"* he'd say. Then Nelson would talk to Jordan as if she understood what he was saying.

Other than Nelson, Jade didn't reach out to anyone. Incoming calls went directly to voicemail. Texts and calls from Sophia, Becca, Marcus, and Renz, went unanswered for weeks. And when Jade called her friends to apologize for not calling, she was relieved to know that they understood.

But Renz was relentless. Renz called Jade often. And when Jade didn't answer his call, he sent her a text. His texts were sincere in nature: *Just checking on you to see how you're doing? When are you coming back up this way? Can I come see you?*

Little did they know, their contact made Jade miss Connor even the more. She yearned for Connor. She wanted to kiss him, cuddle up with him, laugh with him, go on dates with him, and make love with him. She wanted to see Connor play with his daughter, kiss her, change her diaper, feed her, take her to the park, and escort her to school on her first day of kindergarten. But none of that would happen. Instead, Jade had to endure the daunting task of being mommy and daddy.

November was uplifting and surprising. A week before Thanksgiving, Jade and her parents were playing Monopoly. All of a sudden, Jordan spoke for the first time.

"Mama," she squealed.

Jade looked at her parents, they looked at her, they all looked at Jordan and laughed out loud.

"Did she just say what I think she said?" Jade asked.

"She sure did," replied Tanya.

Jade thought it was the most beautiful sound. She wanted to hear those words again and again. A week later, Jordan started crawling. It touched Jade's heart to see Jordan crawl, but she wished that Connor had seen it too.

Jade spent Christmas at home with her family. She thought of Connor and their first Christmas together. Jade wanted to go back to that day and feel Connor's kiss on her lips, and his arms around her belly, but she couldn't. All she had were the memories. After the new year, Justin and Zaria visited more often. Zaria hung out with Jade and tried her best to lift her spirits. Zaria's ploy to make Jade feel better worked for a few days, but eventually, the pain and sorrow of losing Connor crept back into her life.

In April, Renz called and pleaded with Jade to come to Vinny's and enjoy a shrimp scampi on the house. Jade laughed but couldn't resist. She got dressed and drove to Vinny's. After Jade ate, she and Renz talked for a few hours. Renz was concerned and asked Jade how she was doing. Jade was honest and told Renz that she had good days and bad days, that she missed Connor, and that she only left the house to take Jordan to the doctors.

Renz was speechless. He felt sad for Jade and realized that it must have taken a lot of strength for her to come see him.

"Wow, I'm so sorry," said Renz. "I had no idea. You know you could have called me, right? I would have driven down fifty-eight to see you in a heartbeat, girl."

"Thanks, Renz, but all I wanted was to be with Jordan," said Jade.

"I understand," said Renz. "I'm really happy that you accepted my invitation. It's really good to see you and Jordan. She's gorgeous, by the way."

"Thanks," said Jade. "I better get going… Route 58 can be a mess sometimes."

"I'll walk you out," said Renz.

Renz walked Jade to her car. He helped Jade strap Jordan into her car seat, and then he gave Jade a hug goodbye.

"Thanks, Renz," said Jade.

"No problem. Keep in touch," yelled Renz as Jade drove off.

In May, Jade baked Jordan a beautiful strawberry cake for her first birthday. Jade was not in the mood for a big party; she just wanted a small gathering, which consisted of Jordan's immediate family.

Jade decorated the dining room with balloons, a happy first birthday sign, and crepe paper. Everyone wore birthday hats and had paper whistles to celebrate Jordan's birthday. Jade thought about Connor and how happy he would have been to celebrate his daughter's first birthday.

Nelson flew up from Florida for Jordan's birthday. Everyone was happy to see him, including Jordan, and she showed it. When Nelson held Jordan, she laughed and smiled at him.

"I'm so glad you decided to come up," said Jade.

"Wouldn't have missed this for the world," said Nelson.

"Can you do me a favor and record Jordan's special milestone?"

"Absolutely," replied Nelson.

Nelson accepted the task of recording Jordan's birthday. Jade and her family sang "Happy Birthday" to Jordan and blew out the candles for her. Justin played with Jordan as she tried to master the operation of her new toys with her little fingers, Zaria helped Jordan eat her birthday cake, and Jade took lots of pictures of Jordan celebrating her first birthday. Later that night, as Jade laid in bed, she looked at Jordan's pictures and wished that Connor was there with her.

As July approached, Jade was sad and depressed. A year had passed, and Jade wanted to celebrate her first wedding anniversary with Connor, instead, she thought about Connor's funeral and the day he was murdered.

Jade thought about Connor's case and realized that she hadn't heard from Detective Steiner since he visited her last year. She wondered if the detectives found Connor's killer or if the case went cold. The only hope of progress Jade received was when Julia called to speak with her mother. Unfortunately, the conversations ended without any new information regarding Connor's case.

As the days passed, Jade's parents watched movies and played games with her to keep her busy, but most of the time, that didn't work. Jade's mind was elsewhere, and her parents knew it. Her parents invited her to be a third wheel on their date nights, but Jade willfully declined time and time again.

There were days when Jade didn't want to leave her room or see anyone, and that bothered her parents more than anything. Jade's parents felt like they were losing her, and neither one of her parents liked that feeling. Eventually, Jade's parents couldn't bear it anymore and her father decided that something had to be done.

The next morning, Jade's father went to her room and had a heartfelt talk with her.

"Jade, baby, you can't sleep all day," said her father. "That's not good for you or Jordan. Jordan misses her mother and she needs you. She needs to feel your touch, hear your voice, and feel your kisses."

"I can't, Dad. I just can't. I just want to be alone," whined Jade.

"I know that pain all too well, sweetie. When your uncle died…"

Jade was surprised. She looked at her father and said, "My uncle?"

"Yes," replied her father. "You had an uncle. His name was Justin, and he was twelve years old when he died. His death nearly killed my mother and almost tore our family apart. My mother mourned Justin's death to the point that she was unable to move forward. My father felt abandoned and was ready to leave us, but he had to take care of me. I was only ten and surely couldn't take care of myself."

"You never talk about him, Dad."

"I know, but I think about him every day, and I miss him dearly. My brother was always there, like a fixture. He played with me all the time and helped me with my homework. Justin loved to help our mother cook and clean up the house. He was a good boy."

"What happened to him?" Jade asked softly.

"A car hit him," replied her father.

"I'm so sorry, Dad. That had to be awful."

"It was. He died on the way to the hospital. It was devastating for the whole family."

"How did Grandma get over losing her son?"

"My grandmother started taking my mother to church with her every Sunday and Wednesday. My mother hated it, but my grandmother wouldn't let up. After about three months or so, my mother got better. She started talking again, and my dad and I talked about Justin whenever she wanted to. We would look at old family pictures, and my mother would tell us what happened in every photo. It helped her cope with Justin's death, and I enjoyed the stories.

"My mother would stare at me often, not saying a word, just an apologetic stare. I was young, but I knew what she was saying. And when I smiled at her, she would open her arms, and I'd run to her for a hug that we both needed. As the days went by, my mother found purpose for her life, and she decided to live, Jade. She realized that those we love never go away, that they are always with us in spirit."

Tears rolled down Jade's face as she sat up and hugged her father.

"I thank God for you, Daddy," she said.

"Baby, I'm sorry that you're in so much pain. We miss Connor too. Please don't distance yourself from us or your friends. We all love you. Losing a loved one is tragic, but watching your spirit fade away is heartbreaking for me and your mother. We need you. Jordan needs you."

Jade's father kissed her and left her alone in her room. She realized her father was right, he always was.

29

Nelson's internship ended in August and he was considering staying in Miami. His decision would depend on one person, Jade. His feelings for Jade hadn't changed. If anything, his feelings grew stronger with every phone call and video chat.

Nelson thoroughly enjoyed Florida and the work he was doing at the clinic. His friends and colleagues were cool and shared the same interests as he. Marcus visited Nelson a few times throughout the year and had a ball partying in South Beach with him. And then, there was Kendall.

Kendall and Nelson were colleagues and they were attracted to each other. Kendall was beautiful, and in many ways, reminded Nelson of Jade. She was smart, funny, and outgoing. Nelson took Kendall out a few times, but he didn't pursue a relationship with her. He simply enjoyed her company and always had a nice time hanging out with her.

Nelson celebrated the end of his internship with Kendall and a few of his fellow colleagues at Grail's Sports Bar. He sat at the table and watched his friends dance. When Kendall finished dancing, she sat down and talked to Nelson.

"So, Nelson, what are your plans now that the internship is over?" Kendall asked.

"Not really sure," replied Nelson.

"I thought you were taking the job offer here."

"Still thinking about it," said Nelson. "I mean, the salary is great, and it's beautiful down here, but I haven't made up my mind yet."

"I understand," said Kendall. "You should join us in Key West next weekend. You know we're gonna turn it up."

"Can't. I'm surprising a friend for her birthday next weekend," replied Nelson.

"That's sweet of you, Nelson. Why don't you just bring her. We'll show her a good time."

"She lives in Virginia, Kendall."

"Oh, my bad." Kendall laughed.

"What do you have planned?" Nelson asked.

"I plan to celebrate some more and get drunk," replied Kendall.

"You're something else." Nelson laughed.

"Well, if I don't talk to you before your trip, have a safe one," said Kendall. "I'm gonna go dance with Ian…looks like he could use some help."

Nelson laughed. Kendall gave Nelson a hug. Nelson kissed Kendall on her cheek and watched her squeeze her way through the crowded dance floor.

* * *

A week later, Nelson woke up early and drove twelve hours straight to Southampton Virginia. By the time Nelson reached the Virginia state line, he was tired. He went to the hotel, checked in, and went to bed.

The next morning, Nelson showered and got dressed. He splashed on his cologne and threw the bottle of cologne in his duffel bag.

As Nelson packed his bag, and the gifts he bought, he realized how much he missed Jade and how bad he wanted to see her and Jordan.

Nelson was anxious to get to Jade's house and surprise her. He would be early, but he didn't care. He wanted to spend as much time as he could with Jordan before everyone got their hands on her.

Nelson parked in front of the Simpsons' house. He walked to the front door and rang the doorbell. When Jade opened the door and saw Nelson, she was ecstatic. Jade screamed as she leaped in Nelson's arms and gave him a big hug and a kiss.

Nelson was mesmerized when he saw Jade. Jade looked gorgeous in her two-piece, tiger-print bathing suit with a sheer black bikini scarf that hugged her hips.

"Oh my goodness," yelled Jade. "What a great surprise! When did you get in?"

"Last night," replied Nelson.

"Oh wow. You must be tired," said Jade.

"I'm good," said Nelson.

"I'm so glad you came," said Jade. "You look great! That Miami weather is treating you well."

"There was no way I was going to miss your birthday this year. Happy birthday, Jade. This is for you, and this is for Jordan," said Nelson as he handed the gifts to Jade.

"Everyone is out back," said Jade. "I hope you brought your swimming trunks."

Nelson made a funny face, and said, "Oops, sorry."

Jade put the gifts in the family room. Nelson followed Jade to the backyard. When Nelson stepped onto the deck, the sun hit his face like a thick wall of heat. He put on his shades and sat down next to Jade.

Jade introduced Nelson to her cousins Sydney and Michael and to Zaria's sister, Chelsea, and their brother, Elliott.

"Hey, Sydney," said Nelson. "It's good to see you again."

"You too," said Sydney.

"How y'all doing?" Nelson asked as he shook Michael and Elliott's hand.

"We're good," they replied.

"And how are you?" Nelson asked as he looked at Chelsea.

"Fine, and you?" replied Chelsea as she smiled at Nelson.

"What's up, Nelson?" yelled Justin as he climbed out of the pool. He grabbed a towel, dried his face and jumped back into the pool.

"Hey, Justin," yelled Nelson.

"You want something to drink, Nelson?" Jade asked.

"A bottle of water would be great," he replied. "It's hot as hell out here."

"Ain't it," said Chelsea.

Jade walked over to the cooler to get Nelson a bottle of water. When she returned to her seat, Chelsea occupied it.

"I'm going for a swim," said Jade as she put the bottle of water down on the table.

"I'll join you," said Sydney.

"Hold up. Where's my little angel?" Nelson asked.

"Napping," replied Jade. "But she's not that little anymore. Wait until you see her."

Through the slight concealment of his shades, Nelson watched Jade walk to the pool, untie her bikini scarf, and jump into the water. He liked what he saw.

Jade and Sydney chatted with Zaria as she relaxed on the water float and sipped her piña colada. Justin swam over to the girls and splashed water in Zaria's face.

"Justin, what the hell," yelled Zaria. "You got my shades wet!"

"Sorry, baby, but your sister is up to something," said Justin.

Zaria shifted her shades below her eyes to see what Justin was talking about.

"Oh, lordy, she's flirting with Nelson," whispered Zaria.

"Your sister is a cougar," said Justin.

"I know. Thirty years old and thinks she's my age," said Zaria.

"She sure is talking his ear off," said Justin.

Jade turned around to look toward the deck but was interrupted by the arrival of Sophia and Becca.

"Hey, birthday girl," shouted Sophia.

"Happy birthday, Jade," yelled Becca.

"Hey, Sophie and Becca," yelled Jade. "Jump in. The water feels great."

Sophia and Becca dropped their bags on the pool chair, took their shorts off, and jumped into the pool. Michael and Elliott looked at each other and smiled.

"Time for a swim," said Michael.

Jade and Sydney left Justin and Zaria alone and swam over to Kayla, who was relaxing by herself at the other end of the pool.

"Yo, cuz. Who's that guy talking to Chelsea?" Kayla asked.

"That's Nelson," replied Jade.

"Damn, he's fine as hell," said Kayla.

"Girl, you're too much," said Jade.

"Just speaking the truth," said Kayla as she swam away.

Jade glanced over at Nelson and wondered what he and Chelsea were talking about. She watched as Chelsea nudged Nelson with her elbow, and how Chelsea inched her way closer to Nelson and crossed her beautiful legs, and how Nelson smiled when Chelsea's lips stopped moving. *What did she say to him?* Jade thought. And did it even matter, Jade said to herself. Nelson was a single man. He had every right to meet someone and be happy. But Jade couldn't turn away.

"Stop gawking, Jade," said Sydney.

"What are you talking about?" Jade asked.

"You have been watching them for the last ten minutes."

"Girl, get outta here," said Jade.

"I wouldn't worry about that if I were you," said Sydney. "Nelson isn't interested in her."

"How do you know that?" Jade asked.

"I can tell," replied Sydney. "For one thing, he hasn't gotten up to get her a drink yet, which can only mean one thing—he hasn't asked her. If he were interested, he would have asked her if she wanted something to drink by now."

"But like you said, it's only been ten minutes."

"Yeah. Ten minutes too long. Now let's go jump off the diving board," said Sydney.

Jade and Sydney laughed as they got out of the pool and walked over to the diving board.

Nelson heard the girl's laughter and looked in their direction. He watched Jade as she stepped onto the diving board, fixed her bikini bottoms, and jumped into the water. When Nelson smiled, Chelsea thought he was smiling at what she said.

"So then you agree?" Chelsea asked.

"Agree to what?" Nelson asked as he watched Jade.

"That it would be nice if I visited you in Miami," said Chelsea.

Nelson looked at Chelsea. He was surprised at what she said and hoped he hadn't agreed to a visit.

"I'm way too busy with work," said Nelson.

"Well then, maybe another time."

"Yeah," said Nelson as he watched Jade emerge from the water. Nelson continued to watch Jade as she lifted her hands and brushed her curls away from her face. "Gorgeous," he whispered.

Jade got out of the pool and dried herself off. Then she went inside the house to check on Jordan.

"Hey, Mom, is Jordan still sleeping?"

"Nope. She's been up for a while," replied her mother. "I just fed her, and she ate all her food."

"She did? Cool," said Jade. "I'm gonna take her in the pool for a few minutes."

"Sounds like y'all are having a good time. Did I see Nelson out there?"

"Yeah. He drove all the way from Miami to surprise me for my birthday. Wasn't that nice of him?"

"Yes, it was," said her mother.

"When are you and Dad coming out?" Jade asked.

"We'll be out there soon," replied her mother.

Jade took Jordan out of her high chair and carried her outside to the backyard. Nelson and Chelsea were still talking when Jade stepped onto the deck. When Nelson saw Jade holding Jordan, he felt rescued and jumped out of his seat.

"Excuse me, Chelsea," said Nelson as he walked toward Jade.

"There she goes," said Nelson. "Hey, Jordan."

Jordan smiled and waved her little hand. Then she laid her head on Jade's shoulder.

"She recognizes your voice," said Jade.

"She sure does," said Nelson. "She got big."

"Told ya," said Jade. "Are you ready to get in the water, JoJo?"

"Yeah, Mommy," replied Jordan.

"We're going for a dip in the pool. Wanna join us?"

"Sure," replied Nelson.

Nelson walked Jade to the pool and sat down on the pool lounger. He took off his shirt and exposed his bare chest. Jade secretly admired Nelson's upper body, the smooth texture of his tanned, light-brown skin, his muscles that perfectly complimented his chest, and his tiny nipples that looked like chocolate morsels.

Nelson took off his sneakers and put them under the pool lounger. Then he sat down on the edge of the pool and dangled his legs in the water. Nelson held Jordan for a few seconds while Jade got in the pool, then he watched Jade play with Jordan. Jordan laughed as Jade dipped her in and out of the water.

"I think she likes the water," said Nelson.

"She does, a lot," said Jade. "Last week she didn't want to get out of the pool."

"I'll teach her how to swim one day," said Nelson.

"Sounds like a plan. So what's up with you and Chelsea?"

"Nothing. We were just conversating," replied Nelson.

"Looked like you were enjoying the conversation."

"Why you all up in my business, girl?" joked Nelson.

"My bad." Jade laughed.

"You look so beautiful with her, Jade. I wish Connor were here to see this."

"Me too," said Jade.

"C'mere, Jade."

Jade looked at Nelson. She hesitated for a minute before moving closer to him.

"What's up?"

"You remember what I told you when I came over to watch Jordan?"

"Of course," replied Jade.

And Jade did remember. Although it was over a year ago, Jade remembered every word. Jade was flattered that Nelson had feelings for her, but she was in love with Connor then.

Nelson stared into Jade's eyes and said, "I meant every word, Jade. While I was in Florida, I had a lot of time to think, and the only thing that I am unsure of, is whether to accept the job offer."

"They offered you a job!" Jade shouted.

"Yes," said Nelson.

"Nelson, that's great! But why are you undecided? Isn't your dad in Florida?"

"He is, but he's not in Miami. I gotta be honest with you, Jade… I want to be closer to you and Jordan. I missed you a lot, and my feelings for you have gotten stronger."

"Nelson, what do you want me to say? I still miss Connor. I just built up enough strength to take off my engagement ring, and I'm finally able to watch the videos Connor made without crying."

Jade handed Jordan to Nelson and climbed out of the pool.

"Can you watch her while I go get dressed?" Jade stuttered.

"Sure," replied Nelson.

Nelson noticed the change in Jade's demeanor and hoped he didn't upset her.

Jade grabbed a towel off the pool chair and handed it to Nelson. Then Jade wrapped herself in a towel and went inside the house. Nelson sat Jordan on his lap and wrapped the towel around her. He chuckled as Jordan's little body disappeared into the big towel.

Nelson kissed Jordan on her forehead and asked her a question, *"Okay, Jordan, what should I do now?"* Jordan looked at Nelson and made the cutest bubbly sound with her lips. *"So that's all you gotta say."*

* * *

Nelson was happy to be back in Virginia. As soon as he got home, he took a shower, put on a pair of shorts, and got in bed.

He sent Marcus a text to let him know that he was back in Virginia and that he wanted to hang out with him soon. Nelson had a few weeks to decide if he wanted to take the job in Florida. With time on his hands, he figured he would spend that time in Virginia and see Jade and Jordan as much as possible.

As Nelson lay in bed, he surfed the net to find something to do in Southampton. Within minutes, he came across a music festival that the city of Franklin was hosting in two weeks. Nelson figured that would be a good three hours he could spend with Jade. "Let me call her right now," he said.

"Hey, Jade."

"Hey, Nelson," said Jade. "Are you just getting to the hotel?"

"No. I checked out this morning," replied Nelson. "I'm home now. I had a really nice time at your party."

"I'm glad you did. It was really good to see you, Nelson. And thanks for my gift. That was very thoughtful of you."

"So you like it?"

"What! Chance by Chanel. Who wouldn't?"

"So listen, Franklin is having a music festival in two weeks. You should join me."

"I don't know, Nelson. Let me think about it."

"Jade, it's summertime. What is there to think about? You, my friend, need to get out of the house and have some fun."

"What if it rains that day?"

"What if it doesn't?"

"You're right." Jade laughed. "That sounds like fun. I guess I can join you."

"Cool! And don't worry. We'll have a nice time."

"Okay. Good night, Nelson."

30

Two weeks later, Nelson was back at Jade's house. Nelson was especially excited about this visit because he was taking Jade to the music festival and was looking forward to spending time alone with her.

Nelson packed two blankets and a small cooler into his car. In the cooler was Jade's favorite drink in case she got thirsty. He also packed a sweater just in case a chill stirred up in the night air.

When Nelson arrived, Tanya was getting ready to feed Jordan.

"Do you mind if I feed her?" Nelson asked.

"Not at all," replied Tanya.

Tanya handed Jordan's baby plate to Nelson and watched him as he fed Jordan. She admired his gentleness, goofy charisma, and fatherly touch as he interacted with Jordan.

"Hey there, Nelson. How you doing?" Louis asked.

"Good, sir," replied Nelson. "How are you?"

"Great! So how's Miami?"

"Awesome," replied Nelson. "I've been trying to get Jade to come visit, but she won't budge."

Tanya looked at her husband and smiled.

"She likes you, young man," said Louis as he watched Nelson feed Jordan.

"I like her too," said Nelson. "She's adorable."

"So what's this festival y'all going to?" Tanya asked.

"It's a soul music festival where a bunch of local musicians showcase their talents," replied Nelson. "I thought it would be good for Jade to get out of the house and have some fun."

"That's what I've been telling her," said Louis. "All she does is sleep, swim, and take care of Jordan. This outing will do her good. And please don't come back early." Louis laughed.

Tanya and Nelson laughed, which made Jordan laugh.

"What's so funny?" Jade asked as she entered the room.

"Oh nothing," replied her father.

"You look nice," said Nelson. "Ready to go?"

"Yes, I am," replied Jade.

"Great," said Nelson. "Sorry, Mrs. Simpson, but I gotta turn this job back over to you."

"That's fine, dear."

"Good night, Mom and Dad. I'll see y'all later," said Jade.

"Okay, baby. Y'all have fun," said her mother.

Jade gave Jordan a kiss goodbye, and then she grabbed Nelson's arm and pulled him toward the door. "Let's go," she said.

* * *

Nelson carried the cooler and Jade carried the blanket to a grassy area near the stage. He sat the cooler down in the grass and then he helped Jade set the blanket over the grass. Jade kicked off her sandals and sat down. Nelson removed his Sperry's and sat down beside her.

"Looks like it's going to be a good show," said Nelson.

"What makes you say that?"

"Because there's a lot of people here just for the locals," replied Nelson.

"Well, I hope you're right."

"You want something to drink?"

"Not yet," replied Jade. "So how's Chelsea?"

"Who is Chelsea?"

"My party, Zaria's sister, the older woman…"

Nelson laughed at Jade's inquiry and said, "How would I know how she's doing?"

"Well, I talked to Zaria the other day, and she said that Chelsea likes you, a lot."

Before Nelson could respond, his phone rang. He pulled his phone out of his pocket and saw Kendall's name flash on the screen. Nelson raised his index finger, signaling Jade to pause.

"Hey, Kendall, how you doing? I'm good. No, not yet. I will. Okay. Talk to you later."

Nelson hung up and responded to Jade's inquiry.

"Why are you trying to push Chelsea on me?"

"I guess I better not," replied Jade. "Kendall might not like that."

"The festival is starting, girl. Be quiet," joked Nelson.

Jade smiled and nudged Nelson with her elbow. Nelson and Jade listened to the first group, who were actually good. The group consisted of five members, including a female lead singer, who had a beautiful voice. A few people got up to dance as the group performed. Jade and Nelson laughed quietly as they watched an older couple dance off beat.

"Do you know when Mr. and Mrs. Ellis are coming back?"

"Sometime in December," replied Nelson.

"I sure do miss them," said Jade.

"Me too," said Nelson.

"So who's Kendall?"

"One of my colleagues," replied Nelson.

"Are y'all dating?"

"We go out sometimes, but I wouldn't say—"

Jade interrupted Nelson and said, "Good for you, Nelson. I knew you would meet a nice girl one day. Is there a strawberry daiquiri in that cooler?"

"You know it," replied Nelson.

"Cool," said Jade. Jade reached into the cooler and grabbed a strawberry daiquiri. She twisted the cap off and took a long swallow. "Ahh, that's delicious," she said. "You want one?"

"Sure," replied Nelson.

Jade reached into the cooler and grabbed a wine cooler for Nelson. She scooted back to where she was sitting and moved closer to him. "Here you go," said Jade.

"Thanks," said Nelson.

Jade and Nelson drank their wine cooler and watched the various groups perform.

One of the groups serenaded the crowd with a slow song. Nelson wanted to ask Jade to dance, but he didn't want to push. Jade glanced over at Nelson and smiled.

"What?" Nelson asked.

"Wanna dance?"

"Sure," replied Nelson.

Nelson stood up and helped Jade to her feet. He stepped closer to Jade and wrapped his arms around her waist. Then he looked into Jade's eyes and smiled at her. Jade blushed and lowered her head.

"Why are you blushing?" Nelson asked.

Jade shrugged her shoulders in response.

"I want to thank you for inviting me to the festival," said Jade. "You were right, I needed to get out of the house."

"Are you having a good time?" Nelson asked.

"Yes, I am," replied Jade.

"Good. That's what I was hoping for."

When the group finished singing, Jade and Nelson clapped their hands along with the other attendees. Some people yelled out compliments while others whistled in response to the great performance.

After the festival, Nelson drove Jade home. When they arrived at Jade's house, Nelson put his car in park but kept the car running.

"Thanks again," said Jade. "That was fun." Jade leaned over and kissed Nelson on his cheek.

"You're welcome, Jade. I'll call you when I get to the hotel."

"You're not going home?"

"Not tonight," replied Nelson. "I don't wanna take a chance and drive all the way to Williamsburg, so I'm just gonna stay at the Hilton."

"Ah, man. You could have stayed in our spare room," said Jade.

"Maybe next time," said Nelson.

"Okay, good night," said Jade.

Nelson sat in his car until Jade was inside the house. Then he sped off and headed to the hotel. Nelson took a quick shower and got in bed. He tried to relax, but Jade was on his mind. Nelson thought about Jade's kiss and how soft her lips felt on his cheek. He thought about how sexy she looked in her white ruffled top and black shorts. Nelson was aroused and massaged his penis as he thought about Jade, their slow dance, and her kiss. After he relieved himself, he called her.

"Hey, Jade. I'm at the hotel, safe and sound."

"Good. Whatcha doing?"

Nelson chuckled and said, "Lying in the bed, watching television."

"Me too. That was a nice festival," said Jade.

"I thought so too," said Nelson.

"Have you decided on taking the job in Miami?"

"Not yet. I have a few weeks to think about it."

"Does Kendall live in Florida?"

"Yes. Why?"

"Then your decision should be easy."

"I wish it were that easy," said Nelson.

"Well, how do you feel about her, Nelson?"

"She's cute, nice, witty, and smart, like someone else I know," he joked.

"Nelson, I'm serious. Why isn't she your girlfriend?"

"You know why, Jade. And you also know how I feel about you. I just need to know how you feel about me."

"I wish I knew, Nelson. But what I do know is that you have been a blessing to me and Jordan, and I love you for that."

"I love you too, Jade. I'll call you tomorrow."

"Okay," said Jade.

Jade hung up the phone and turned off the television. She laid in bed and thought about the lovely evening she had with Nelson. He didn't make any moves on her or implore any flirtatious behavior. He was a gentleman.

She wondered if Kendall had nice dates with Nelson. Did he treat her nice? Did his soft lips kiss her good night? Did his sexy voice make her melt? Jade knew all that to be true because she had experienced it for herself.

31

Early Saturday morning, Tanya and Louis went to Kroger's to refill the pantry before their vacation. In a week, Jade's parents were going to the Bahamas, and they wanted to make sure Jade had enough food in the house while they were away.

When Jade woke up, she fed Jordan. Suddenly, Jade felt an overwhelming presence fill her body. She felt Connor's spirit and knew that he was there with her. As Jade's eyes filled with water, the doorbell rang. Jade wiped her eyes and went to answer the door.

"Hey, Nelson, come in," said Jade. "You're right on time. I just fed JoJo, and she's ready to play."

"Good. Where is she?"

"In the family room," replied Jade.

Nelson made his way to the family room.

"You look so cute," said Nelson as he lifted Jordan out of her walker.

"Dada," said Jordan. Nelson was flabbergasted. He looked at Jade and chuckled. "Did she just say dada?" Nelson asked.

"She did," replied Jade. "She thinks you're her daddy."

"Oh, how I wish that were so," whispered Nelson.

"Where's your Mom and Dad?"

"Grocery shopping," replied Jade.

"Oh," said Nelson.

Nelson sat Jordan on his lap and rattled her toy in his hands. Jordan laughed as she reached for her toy. Jade grabbed her phone and hit the record button.

"JoJo, look at Mommy," she said. "Smile."

Nelson and Jordan looked at Jade and smiled. Jade tapped the camera button on her phone and took a picture.

"Make sure you send me that picture," said Nelson.

"Sending it to you now," said Jade.

"Thanks," said Nelson.

Nelson put Jordan back in her walker and continued to play with her. Jade watched him as he made funny faces and played peek-a-boo with Jordan. Jordan laughed uncontrollably.

"You're good with her," said Jade.

"She makes it easy for me. So Jade, I was thinking. When your parents get back, we should take a ride down to Lake Gaston."

"Lake Gaston. That's in North Carolina, Nelson."

"Yeah, I know. But it's not far from here at all."

"What do people do there?"

"Have fun," replied Nelson. "I reserved a boat tour for us."

"Okay," said Jade. "That sounds like fun."

When Jade's parents got home, she helped her mother put the groceries away. After that, Jade took Jordan upstairs and changed her diaper. Then she grabbed her sweater out of the closet and went downstairs with Jordan in her arms.

"Okay, I'm ready," said Jade.

"Have fun at the lake," said her mother.

"How'd you know about that?" Jade asked.

"Nelson just told us," replied her father. "We'll take care of Jordan. You just go and have fun, baby."

"Okay. Thanks, guys. See y'all later."

"See you later, sweetheart," said her mother.

As Nelson drove to Lake Gaston, he turned on the radio and started singing along to Joe's "I Wanna Know." Jade smiled as Nelson belted out the lyrics.

"I sound good, don't I?" said Nelson.

"Yep." Jade laughed.

Jade lowered the window halfway and leaned her head back. She closed her eyes and breathed in the cool September air. Nelson looked at Jade and admired the way her curls looked like streams of beautiful ribbon blowing in the air. He gently touched her curls with the back of his hand, but his moment of intimacy was interrupted when her phone rang.

Jade looked at her phone and was surprised to see that Renz was calling her. She hadn't talked to Renz since visiting him at Vinny's. Sure, they exchanged a few texts since then, but they hadn't communicated verbally in five months. But today, Jade wanted to talk to Renz because texting him just wasn't the same as hearing his voice.

"Hi, Renz, how are you doing?"

"Okay," replied Renz. "I was just thinking about you. Vinny's isn't the same without you, girl. How's Jordan?"

"She's fine," replied Jade. "I want to apologize for not answering your calls. That was selfish of me. How's your family doing?"

"No need to apologize," said Renz. "And they're doing okay. No word from my cousin yet, but other than that, we're good."

"Sorry to hear that," said Jade.

"Thanks. I just wanted to call and see how you were doing. You sound great."

"I'm doing better and thanks for calling," said Jade.

"No problem, Jade. I'll talk to you later."

"Okay, Renz. Talk to you later."

Jade smiled as she disconnected the call and realized that she had missed his voice.

"Who's Renz?" Nelson asked.

"My friend from Vinny's."

"The pizza joint by your old place?"

"Yeah," replied Jade.

"What's going on between you two?"

"Nothing," replied Jade. "He's just a friend."

"Yeah right." Nelson chuckled. "That didn't sound like a 'just a friend' conversation to me," said Nelson.

"I'm serious." Jade laughed. "I haven't talked to Renz in months. We text each other from time to time, and that's all."

Nelson smiled at Jade's attempt to make him think otherwise. He thought it was kind of Jade to thumb down whatever feelings she had for Renz. Little did she know, Nelson didn't care how she felt about Renz one way or the other. Nelson had plans to win Jade's heart, and there was no way he was going to let a pizza boy get in the way of that.

When they arrived at Lake Gaston, Nelson parked near the pier. He and Jade got out of the car and walked over to a small white shack with a huge square opening that served as a window for the boat attendant.

"Hello. I'm Nelson. I have a boat tour reserved with Brandon."

"Oh, Nelson. Brandon tried to call you, dude. He had an emergency and had to leave, so we had to cancel your reservation."

"What! Well, is there anyone else to take us on the tour?"

"Yeah, but he's out on a tour now," replied the attendant. "If you want to wait, you can. He'll be back in about forty-five minutes."

"I guess that's up to her," said Nelson as he looked at Jade. "You want to wait or do something else?"

"Let's do something else," replied Jade.

"I guess we're not waiting." Nelson laughed as he looked at the attendant. "How do I get my refund?"

"I just need the card you used to reserve the tour, and we'll credit your account," replied the attendant.

Nelson handed the attendant his credit card. He looked at Jade with sadness in his eyes and wondered what they were going to do now that the boat tour was cancelled.

"Don't look so sad. We'll find something to do," said Jade.

"I'm sorry. I just wanted you to have a good time," said Nelson. "I guess we can walk around the lake."

"That sounds good to me," said Jade.

Nelson and Jade walked along the lake, taking pleasure in the scenery and the beautiful houses erected on the other side of the lake.

"Jade, I had planned to tell you this on the boat tour, but since that part of my plan got squashed, I guess I can tell you now."

"You accepted the job offer," blurted Jade.

"Damn, girl. How'd you know?"

"Lucky guess," replied Jade as she shrugged her shoulders. "When do you leave?"

"Next month," he replied.

"So soon?"

"Duty calls."

"I'm happy for you, Nelson. Congratulations," said Jade as she gave Nelson a hug.

"Thanks, Jade."

"So what are we going to do now?" Jade asked.

"Not sure," replied Nelson. "I wish I kept my Frisbees."

Jade laughed and said, "Let's play tag. You're it," yelled Jade as she tapped Nelson on his shoulder and ran down the lake's waterline.

Nelson watched Jade as she ran away. After a minute or two, he kicked off his Sperrys and ran after her. Nelson picked up his speed and caught up to Jade. Then he grabbed Jade from behind and slowed her down.

"Gotcha," he yelled.

Jade laughed as she tried to free herself from Nelson's grip. She grabbed Nelson's hands and tried to remove them from her waist. In doing so, she tripped over her feet, and she and Nelson fell.

Nelson fell on his back, and Jade fell on top of him, her face facing his. In the joy of the moment, they laughed at each other. As their laughter dwindled, Jade stared at Nelson and wondered what he was thinking. Nelson looked at Jade and held her tighter, not wanting to let her go.

Jade was having fun, and before she knew it, she pressed her lips against Nelson's lips. Nelson didn't resist. He responded by kissing Jade back. When Jade realized what she was doing, she immediately sat up and apologized.

"Sorry, Nelson. I shouldn't have done that."

"It's okay, Jade."

"No, Nelson, it's not. You're with Kendall, and I don't want to get in the middle of that."

"In the middle of what? Kendall and I are friends."

"You make me feel like everything is okay."

"Because everything *is* okay, Jade."

"Then why do I feel like this is wrong? Like I'm cheating on Connor?"

"Jade, don't say that. We're going to miss Connor for the rest of our lives. That doesn't mean we have to stop being happy."

"So, big psychology man," shouted Jade. "Would that require kissing you?"

"That's not what I'm saying, Jade. You once told me that Connor would want us to keep living. It was hard for me to believe you then, but I believe you now. You were right. We can't punish ourselves for what happened. Connor wouldn't want us to do that."

"I'm ready to go home. Please take me home." Jade got up and started walking toward the parking lot.

"Hold up, Jade. Let me put on my shoes," shouted Nelson.

Jade stopped walking and waited for Nelson. When Nelson caught up to her, they walked quietly to the car.

Neither one of them uttered a word on the way home. Nelson wanted to talk to Jade, but he figured he had said all that he could say. Nelson knew Jade was still hurting, and he wanted to help her, but he didn't know how. What Nelson did know, was that he loved Jade, and he had to stop convincing her that she deserved to be happy.

When Nelson arrived at Jade's house, he put his car in park and turned off the engine.

"I just want to say this, and then I'll leave," he said. "I'm sorry that you're still hurting, but you have got to find joy in your sorrow. Please don't let your spirit die, Jade. You have way too much to live for. I just wish you knew that too."

Nelson looked at Jade, wiped her tears away, and whispered, "I love you, Jade Simpson."

Jade jumped out of the car and rushed inside the house.

She went straight upstairs to her bedroom and sat on the edge of the bed. She thought about Nelson and what he said to her. His words resonated within her spirit and she realized that Nelson was right. *Connor would want me to live and be happy. But how?*

32

A week after visiting Lake Gaston, Jade was feeling depressed. She felt bad for having a good time with Nelson. How was that fair to Connor? How could she kiss another man? Jade was fighting her feelings and needed to talk to her mother about how she felt.

"Hey, Mom," said Jade as she opened the door. "Looks like you're all packed and ready to go."

"Just about," said her mother. "I've been meaning to ask you about your trip last week. How was it?"

"It was nice. But something happened, and I don't know how to feel about it."

"Come sit down and talk to me, baby. What's going on with you?"

Jade sat down and said, "My chest feels like there's a big knot in it, and I just want it untied. And on top of that, I have feelings for someone, but I feel like I'm betraying Connor. I'm scared to let go, Mom. What if my heart gets broken again?"

"Baby, the loss of someone dear to us is never easy. You're going to miss Connor forever but you can't stop living, baby. Our feelings to love and care for others is natural, and you should not feel bad about having feelings for someone else. You're lovable, Jade, and you are deserving of love.

"Now, about Nelson. He loves you. Don't be afraid to love again, sweetheart. Connor wouldn't want that. Connor would want you to enjoy life and share your love with someone special."

"How'd you know I was talking about Nelson?"

"Baby, love is action and Nelson has been visiting you almost every weekend since he returned from Florida."

"But Nelson is moving back to Florida next month, and I haven't told him how I feel."

"Then I guess you better get busy," said her mother.

"Thanks," said Jade as she gave her mother a hug. "I love you."

"I love you too, baby."

"Good night, Mom. Have a safe flight tomorrow."

Jade went to her room, gave Jordan a goodnight kiss, and got ready for bed. As Jade laid in bed, she thought about what her mother said, then she closed her eyes and fell into a deep sleep.

It was her wedding day, and as Ava predicted, it was fabulous. Everything was just as she and Connor planned. The church was decorated lovely. The flower arrangements were beautiful. Her wedding dress was gorgeous, and it looked amazing on her. Her bridesmaids looked beautiful in their lavender dresses. Connor looked GQ handsome in his white five-piece tailcoat tux with a lavender bow tie and cummerbund. The groomsmen looked equally handsome in their black tuxedos. Nelson stood tall as Connor's best man. Mariah was the most beautiful flower girl anyone had ever seen, and Avery was the handsomest ring bearer ever. Jade stared at Connor as her father walked her down the aisle. And when she saw Connor wipe away a tear, her eyes watered. When it was time to exchange vows, Connor vowed to love Jade and Jordan forever, that he would honor, respect, and cherish Jade every day of his life.

"Meeting you, Jade, was the best thing that ever happened to me," he said. "You and Jordan bring me so much joy. You are it for me, Jade. There will never be anyone else. I want to share the rest of my life with you."

And then they kissed. It *was* perfect!

After they consummated their union, Connor surprised Jade with what he said next.

"Baby, I know we just got married, but I want you to know something." Connor looked into Jade's eyes as he spoke. "Always love, Jade, because you're good at it!"

Jade woke up with enough vigor to move a mountain. Her heart was beating fast, and she felt like a ton of bricks had been lifted off her chest. Connor's words untied the guilt she felt for having feelings for Nelson. Jade was at peace and finally able to breathe.

* * *

Jade planned to spend the entire weekend playing with Jordan and catching up on her TCM movies. Jordan kept Jade busy during the day. She ran around the house, played with her toys, and watched cartoons.

When it was time for Jordan's nap, Jade watched a movie. After the movie, Jade was bored and decided to bake some chocolate chip cookies. Once the cookies were in the oven, Jade watched another movie. She opted for a Denzel flick. As Jade watched *Training Day*, she glanced at her phone and hoped that it would ring and she would hear Nelson's voice on the other end, but her phone didn't ring.

Nelson hadn't called Jade since their visit to Lake Gaston, and Jade didn't blame him. She was confused about her feelings, and Nelson deserved better.

Maybe he went back to Florida early, thought Jade. If that were the case, she would understand. Nelson had a good opportunity waiting for him in Miami. Not only that, Kendall was there, and Nelson could move on with whatever plans he had with her and be happy.

Jade took the cookies out of the oven and placed them on the counter. She checked her phone again. No missed calls from Nelson. Jade couldn't stand it anymore. She picked up her phone and called Nelson. She heard Nelson's sexy voicemail greeting and left him a message.

An hour later, Nelson called Jade back.

"Hey, Jade. Sorry I missed your call. I was sleeping. Is everything okay?"

"Yes," replied Jade. "I just called you to apologize."

"For what?"

"For the way I treated you at the lake. I was wrong for what I said to you, and I apologize."

"Apology accepted," said Nelson. "So what's up with you and JoJo?"

"Nothing." Jade laughed. "JoJo is napping, and I'm watching movies. What's up with you?"

"Not much. Just washing clothes and getting things ready for Florida," replied Nelson.

Jade smiled. He was still in Virginia, and she was happy about that. This was her opportunity to see Nelson one last time before he went back to Florida. This was her chance to tell Nelson how she felt about him.

"Cool. Well, listen. I was wondering if you wanted to come over. I made some chocolate chip cookies."

Nelson laughed. "I like peanut butter cookies though."

"You would," said Jade. "I can run to the store and get you peanut butter cookies."

"No." Nelson laughed. "It's all good."

"So are you coming over?"

"Uh," sighed Nelson. "By the time I finish washing clothes and packing, it's gonna be close to five. And Southampton is well over an hour away, Jade."

"I understand. Well, I guess I'll talk to you later." Jade hung up the phone. Two minutes later, her phone rang.

"Hey, you hung up on me." Nelson laughed. "I'll see you in an hour or so."

"Okay. We'll be here," said Jade.

Jade was so excited that she clapped her hands and jumped up and down. She was looking forward to seeing Nelson and now that he was coming over, she could tell him how she felt before he left for Florida.

Nelson arrived about an hour and twenty minutes later. He looked handsome in his black jeans and gray polo shirt.

"Thanks for coming over and keeping me company," said Jade.

"Keeping you company. Where are your parents?"

"In the Bahamas," replied Jade.

"Nice," said Nelson. "Where's Jordan?"

"In the family room," replied Jade. "She woke up a few minutes ago, and she's waiting for you to play with her."

Jordan was in her playpen, playing with her toys. When Nelson saw her, he smiled, picked her up, and kissed her on the cheek.

"Hey, JoJo," said Nelson.

"Hi," said Jordan.

"So you made chocolate chip cookies?"

"I sure did," replied Jade. "Let me go get them."

Jade went into the kitchen to get the cookies. When she returned, Nelson was helping Jordan walk around the family room. Jade put the plate of cookies down, grabbed her phone, and hit the record button.

"Y'all look cute," she said.

"She's doing all the work," said Nelson. "Ain't that right, JoJo." Jordan laughed and said something neither one of them understood.

"Do you like the old black-and-white movies?"

"Only the gangster ones," replied Nelson.

"Well, I was about to watch *The Maltese Falcon*. Wanna watch it?"

"Sure," replied Nelson.

Nelson put Jordan in her playpen. Jade dimmed the lights, started the movie, and sat down on the couch with Nelson. After the movie, Jade fed Jordan and gave her a quick bath.

"Are you hungry?" Jade asked.

"Actually, I am," replied Nelson.

"Me too. What do you have a taste for?"

"Chinese food," replied Nelson.

"Cool. What do you want?"

"Shrimp Egg Foo Yung," replied Nelson.

Jade called the Chinese restaurant and placed the order. She added a small pint of shrimp fried rice and ribs to the order.

"The food will be here in twenty minutes," said Jade.

"How much?" Nelson asked.

"I don't know," replied Jade. "My parents left me some cash though. I'm sure I'll have enough."

"I'll take care of it, Jade."

"Thanks, Nelson. I'm glad that you came over because I wanted to talk to you about something."

"I'm listening," said Nelson.

Jade put the television on mute and looked at Nelson. Nelson was all ears and ready to hear what Jade had to say.

"Nelson, I know you're leaving for Florida soon, but I want you to know something…I have feelings for you, but I'm not ready for a relationship. You have been such a great friend, and I appreciate that. I really do. And I couldn't let you leave without telling you how I feel."

"Jade, you don't have to explain anything to me," said Nelson. "I know you need more time. Maybe my time in Florida will give you some time to think about what you want. And if you just want to be friends, I'll be okay with that. You already know how I feel about you, and I don't want to push or make you feel uncomfortable. So when you decide, just let me know."

"Thank you, Nelson."

Nelson paid for the Chinese food when it arrived. Jade made their plates, and she and Nelson sat down in the family room and ate their food while they watched *Scarface*. After the movie, Nelson was ready to go home.

"It's late, Jade. I better get going."

"Thanks for keeping us company. Do you want to take some cookies home?"

"Nah, I'm good." Nelson laughed. Nelson stood up and looked at Jade. He wanted to hold her and tell her that he loved her, but she already knew that.

Jade wasn't ready for Nelson to leave. She looked at Nelson with a compelling stare that melted his heart.

"What is it?" he asked.

"Can you stay?"

"Jade, I gotta get home and finish packing," he replied.

"Please stay," said Jade. "I want you to stay. Will you stay?"

Nelson heard the loneliness in Jade's voice and felt sorry for her. He sat back down and gave her a hug.

"Sure, I can stay," replied Nelson.

Jade turned off the television. Nelson picked up Jordan and followed Jade upstairs to her room. He laid Jordan down on the bed and followed Jade down the hall to the guest room.

"Here you go," said Jade. "There's a full bath in here just in case you want to take a shower."

"This is nice. Thanks, Jade."

Jade gave Nelson a hug and went to her bedroom. She took a quick shower and put on a pair of shorts and a T-shirt. Jade stared at the ceiling and smiled as she thought about Nelson.

She thought about how much fun they had at the festival and how much she enjoyed slow dancing with him. Jade thought about the kiss at the lake and how soft his lips were. She thought about the times Nelson told her how he felt about her and how sincere he was with his feelings. Nelson's words made Jade feel special, and she wanted to be next to him.

Nelson took off his clothes and got in bed. As he laid in the dark room, he thought about Florida and how the move would be a big change from living in Virginia. There was so much more to do in Florida, and he liked that. He also liked the fact that he would be able to spend more time with his family. As Nelson thought about his family, he heard a knock on the door. He jumped out of the bed and opened the door. To his surprise, stood Jade with an adoring look on her face.

Jade smiled and tucked her bottom lip under her teeth. She pulled on Nelson's undershirt until his lips met hers. Jade's kiss was intense. Nelson shut the door and kissed Jade back with a force that told her he wanted her too.

33

Nelson always looked forward to visiting Jade, but today's visit was bittersweet. Come Monday, Nelson was heading back to Florida to start his new job and he was excited about that.

When Nelson arrived, he and Jade hugged and kissed each other's cheek. Then Jade took his coat and hung it in the coat closet near the front door.

"We just started playing Yahtzee. Wanna play?"

"Sure. I hope y'all aren't sore losers."

Jade laughed and punched Nelson in the arm.

Nelson sat down with Jade and her family and played two games of Yahtzee. Tanya won the first game, and Nelson won the second game.

"Nice job, Nelson," said Louis.

"Thank you, sir."

"I'm heading to the kitchen," said Jade. "Does anyone want anything?"

"We're good, baby," replied her mother.

Jade went to the kitchen to get a glass of iced tea and chips. As she returned to the family room, her phone rang.

"Hey, Renz. How you doing?"

"Okay," he replied.

"You sound upset. What's wrong?"

"I have something to tell you, Jade. Are you sitting down?"

"Yes, I am," replied Jade.

"I just left the hospital," said Renz.

"The hospital. What happened?"

Renz confessed, "My cousin hurt Connor, and I'm so sorry, Jade."

Jade yelled into the phone, "What are you saying, Renz?"

Jade's parents and Nelson stopped what they were doing and looked at her. Jade put her phone on speaker and placed it on the table.

"My cousin Lucas...he robbed and shot Connor," replied Renz. "I'm so sorry, Jade. I feel terrible."

Jade and her family were shocked by what they were hearing. Jade's father didn't understand why Renz was calling her and not the police.

"How do you know your cousin killed Connor?" Jade asked.

"Because I beat his ass until he told me the truth about the diamond earring he was wearing."

Jade started to cry. She had no idea Connor's earring was taken during the shooting. Jade's mother sat down next to her and consoled her.

"Renz, you never met Connor, so how do you even know about his earring?"

"That night I brought you your credit card, remember. I saw Connor's earring in the picture when I was at your place. I could tell it was expensive and my cousin can't afford a diamond earring like that."

"Excuse me," said Louis. "This is Jade's father. Did you call the police?"

"Yes, sir. I called them when I got to the hospital with Lucas. They met me there and took my statement. And I wanted to tell Jade what I told them."

"And what is that?" Louis asked.

"That my cousin didn't act alone. He's young and a good kid. Lucas has an older sister named Lisa. I didn't see the connection between Lisa and Connor until the detective told me where Connor worked, and I knew Lisa had worked there before. Now I know why she disappeared last year. We still don't know where she is, sir, but Lucas told me that Lisa got him to rob and shoot Connor."

"I want to thank you for what you did," said Louis. "I know it took a lot for you to turn your cousin in to the police. I...we truly appreciate it."

"Thank you, sir. Please tell Jade that I am very, very, sorry. Lucas has never done anything like this before. I feel terrible knowing that my family is to blame for Jade's sorrow. Please tell Jade that I am terribly sorry."

"I will. And thank you," said Louis.

"You're welcome, sir."

"I gotta get out of here," cried Jade.

"Let's go get some air," said Nelson. "We'll be back, Mr. Simpson."

Nelson helped Jade with her coat. Then he grabbed his coat and walked out of the house with Jade. Nelson helped Jade into his car. He got in the driver's seat and rolled down the windows to let the fresh air in. He started the car and drove quietly through the city.

"I need something to drink," said Jade.

"No problem. I'll stop at 7-Eleven." Five minutes later, Nelson pulled into the 7-Eleven parking lot.

Before Nelson got out of the car, he grabbed Jade's hand and said, "Everything is going to be okay, Jade."

"Thanks, Nelson."

"Maybe I should stay in Virginia through the holidays."

"No, no," cried Jade. "You have a job waiting for you. I'll be fine."

"The job can wait," said Nelson. "You need me to be here, Jade."

"Can we talk about this later?"

"Sure. I'll be right back," replied Nelson.

Alone in the car, Jade allowed her tears to fall and cover her face. She checked her pockets for a napkin, but her pockets were empty. Jade opened the glove compartment and saw what looked to be a napkin. She reached into the glove compartment and grabbed it. What Jade thought was a napkin turned out to be a letter with the words "best man speech" written on it. Jade turned on the interior lights and read the letter.

To my brother, C. There isn't much to say to a guy that has everything. But you know me, I always have something to say. I thank God for you every day, my brother. You and your family took me in when I was at my deepest sorrow, and I will be forever grateful to you and your family. So, on today, I want to say, to Connor and to Jade, that I am overjoyed that God connected your souls. The love that I see in you both can only come from one source, and that source is our heavenly Father. Bro, you have found someone that makes you happy, someone that you can laugh with, cry with, and have fun with, if you know what I mean, and that's special. Your love for each other is unconditional, and that kind of love will last forever. I pray God blesses this union with an abundance of wealth, health, and rugrats. To Connor and Jade, I love you both!

Jade read Nelson's speech over and over. She thought it was the most beautiful thing she had ever read. And even though it brought back memories of Connor, she loved Nelson's speech all the same.

When Nelson got in the car, he looked at Jade and noticed she had been crying. Nelson didn't say anything. He leaned over to console Jade, and that's when he saw it; his speech to Connor and Jade, in her hands, riddled with remnants of her tears.

"Oh my goodness, Jade. I'm so sorry. I forgot..."

"It's beautiful, Nelson. Your words, they're beautiful. May I keep this?"

"Sure. Of course," replied Nelson.

"Thank you," said Jade as she wiped her tears away.

Nelson started the car and shifted the gear to reverse. Then he hesitated, put the car in park, and turned off the engine.

"What's wrong?" Jade asked.

"I need to tell you something," replied Nelson. Nelson paused and said, "I knew about Lisa."

Jade was outraged. "You what!" she yelled. "Why didn't you do something?"

"I tried to, Jade. Connor showed me her texts. She threatened him, and I told him to go to the police. I should have done more, and I'm sorry I didn't."

"Was Connor seeing her?"

"No. Hell no," replied Nelson. "That girl was fucking crazy, and Connor didn't want anything to do with her."

"I can't believe you didn't tell me," cried Jade.

"I know. I'm sorry. I should have told you all this a long time ago," said Nelson.

Jade stared at Nelson with tears in her eyes. Then after a moment of silence, Jade and Nelson hugged and cried in each other's arms.

34

Christmas Day

It was Christmas, and Jade was in high spirits. Jade invited her closest friends to spend Christmas with her and her family. She invited Nelson and couldn't wait for him to arrive. Jade also invited Connor's parents, in hopes that they were back from Italy and available to spend Christmas with her and her family.

Jade and Zaria helped her mother cook Christmas dinner. On the menu was shrimp, fried chicken, honey-glazed ham, candied yams, collard greens, baked macaroni and cheese, lasagna, stuffing, peach cobbler, sweet potato pie, red velvet cake, and peanut butter cookies.

After Jade helped her mother set the dining room table, she took a shower and got dressed. She dressed Jordan in a beautiful red-and-black velvet dress. Jade put matching hair accessories in Jordan's curly ponytails and carried her downstairs.

"There goes my little princess," shouted Justin. "The prettiest girl in the room."

Jordan responded in her baby talk language that made Jade and Justin laugh. Justin made a silly face which made Jordan laugh. Then Jordan opened her arms for Justin to hold her.

"You're gonna spoil her rotten," said Jade.

"Uncles are supposed to spoil their nieces, girl."

"Remember you said that," said Jade.

As the guests arrived, Jade guided them into the family room where the drinks and appetizers awaited them.

Sophia, Becca, and Marcus drove down to Southampton together. Jade hadn't seen Sophia and Becca since her birthday, and she was elated when they arrived. She hadn't seen Marcus since Connor's funeral, and when she hugged him, she held onto him longer than usual.

"You look great, Jade," said Marcus.

"I've missed you, Marcus," said Jade. "Thanks for coming."

"Anytime," he said.

When Nelson arrived, Jade was overjoyed. Jade hadn't seen Nelson since October, and she had missed him tremendously. But what Jade wanted more than anything was for Connor to be there with her and Jordan. Jade and Nelson hugged each other tight. Nelson heard Jade sniffle and knew she was thinking about Connor.

"I wish Connor were here too," he whispered.

Jade led Nelson to the family room where they joined their friends at the appetizer table. The atmosphere was calm. Christmas music blared through the house, and the combination of all the food left a sweet aroma in the air.

Jade was talking to her friends when she felt Connor's presence. She smiled and knew that Connor was there with her. As her eyes began to tear up, she excused herself.

"Excuse me. I'll be right back," said Jade.

"Are you okay?" Becca asked.

"Yes," replied Jade.

When Jade turned around to go to the bathroom, she saw Connor's parents standing in the foyer.

"Mr. and Mrs. Ellis," yelled Jade as she ran to the foyer and hugged Connor's parents. "I'm so happy y'all made it."

"So are we, sweetie," said Julia.

"Let me get your coats, and then you gotta come see how big Jordan is."

Jade hung their coats in the closet. She grabbed Julia's hand and led her into the family room.

Julia looked around the room and saw all of Connor's friends chatting and having a wonderful time. And when Connor's friends saw Julia, they rushed to her side and embraced her.

"It's so good to see you," they all said.

"It's good to see all of you too," said Julia. "And is that Jordan I see playing with Justin?"

"It sure is," replied Jade.

"My, my, my, she's adorable," said Julia.

"Merry Christmas, Mr. and Mrs. Ellis," said Justin. "You want to hold her?"

"Absolutely," said Julia.

Justin handed Jordan to Julia. Jordan smiled as she looked at her grandmother.

"Mama," said Jordan.

Julia smiled and stared at Jordan for a long time. Jade knew she missed Connor. Everyone did. But Jade was happy that Connor's parents were there because she had missed them too.

"I missed y'all so much," cried Jade. "And thank you for the card. It was beautiful."

"We missed you too," said Julia.

"How was Italy?" Jade asked.

"Lovely," replied Gordon.

"I'm sure it was," said Jade.

"Excuse me," said Tanya as she stepped into the family room. "Before we eat, I just want to welcome you all to our home. We're all family here, and I want you all to have a good time and make yourselves at home. And if you need anything, anything at all, just let me know."

Tanya glanced around the room and saw Connor's parents playing with Jordan. She walked over to Julia and Gordon to personally welcome them to her home.

"Merry Christmas, Julia and Gordon. Welcome to our home. How was Italy?"

"Thank you, Tanya. Italy was great, but it's good to be home. And look at Jordan. She's growing so fast."

"She sure is," said Tanya. "Gordon, come with me. Louis is waiting for you."

"Jade, I want to thank you for letting Jordan stay with us after Connor's funeral. That was very thoughtful of you. I needed a part of my son with me, and having Jordan around helped me cope, so I thank you."

"You're welcome. I hope she didn't give you too much trouble."

"Are you kidding me?" said Julia. "She was an angel."

"I want JoJo to know her grandparents. The best of Connor came from you and Mr. Ellis, and I want Jordan to know that."

"Sweetheart, she will. I have so many stories to tell Jordan about her daddy," said Julia.

"I gotta tell ya though. Being a mother is a full-time job. Jordan keeps me busy. But the best part of my day is spending time with her."

"She is precious," said Julia.

"Okay, family," yelled Tanya. "It's time to eat. Julia, come with me, sweetheart."

Everyone headed to the dining room. The food looked great and smelled delicious. Once everyone sat down, they all held hands and Louis prayed. After Louis prayed, he stood up to give a toast.

"Get your wineglasses," Louis shouted. "It's time to toast it up. I thank God for each of you. It is truly a blessing to have you all here celebrating Christmas with my family. Gordon and Julia, I know last year was hard for you, so I want to take a moment and honor Connor who I know is here with us in spirit."

"To Connor," said Louis.

"To Connor," said everyone in unison.

"Thank you for that, Louis," said Gordon. "We appreciate it."

"We miss Connor too," said Louis.

"I know," said Gordon. Gordon looked at his wife and grabbed her hand.

Jade was surrounded by love. She smiled as Gordon kissed his wife and as her mother blew a kiss to her father. Jade watched Justin and Zaria whisper sweet nothings to one another, and she laughed quietly as she saw Sophia watching Jordan flip her lips with her fingers. She saw Becca smile as Michael chatted with her. Jade shook her head as Sydney and Kayla raced to finish their wine while Elliott cheered them on. She glanced at Marcus, who was looking at his watch, and finally, Jade looked at Nelson, who was staring at her.

Jade dabbed her eyes with a napkin. Nelson gently squeezed her hand and said, "Your father is right. Connor's spirit is here."

Suddenly, Zaria jumped up from her seat, surprising everyone.

"You going somewhere?" Justin asked.

"No," replied Zaria. "I have something to say. Justin, Mom, Dad…" Zaria paused and took a deep breath. "We're pregnant!"

"Oh my goodness," yelled Tanya. "Congratulations!"

Tanya jumped up, rushed over to Zaria, and gave her a hug and a kiss. Everyone congratulated Zaria and Justin. Justin stood up and shared an emotional hug with his wife.

"Thank you for the best Christmas gift ever," whispered Justin.

"Anyone else have any good news to share on this Christmas Day?"

"Yes," replied Gordon. "Detective Steiner called us last week and said they have two people in custody. And Julia and I thank God for that!"

"Amen," said Louis.

"Amen," shouted the guests.

"Gordon, after we eat, I got something to show you out back."

"Sounds good, Louis."

* * *

After dinner, everyone helped themselves to dessert. When Jade finished her dessert, she and her cousins cleaned off the dining room table and then tackled the kitchen.

Louis took Gordon out to the backyard, and they disappeared into Louis' man-cave. Tanya kept Julia company as they watched television and played with Jordan.

Nelson and Marcus went outside and helped Justin and Michael start the fire pit. When Jade finished cleaning the kitchen, she joined her friends in the backyard. Becca and Michael were sitting together and talking among themselves. Sophia was sitting with Marcus, and Zaria was snuggled up next to Justin, already wrapped up in a blanket. Nelson was sitting alone.

"Where my cousins at?" Justin asked.

"They wanted to stay inside and chill with Elliott," replied Jade. "You guys hogged all the seats, I see."

"I saved you a seat right here, Jade," said Nelson.

"Why, thank you, Nelson," said Jade as she sat down next to him.

"Yo, Nelson," yelled Justin. "How's Miami?"

"Nice," replied Nelson. "I'm still trying to get your sister to come visit, but she keeps turning me down. When are you and Zaria coming to visit?"

"Soon, and definitely before my son is born," replied Justin.

"I hear ya," said Nelson. "I'll show you both a good time."

"I'm sure you will," said Justin.

"Oh, he definitely will," said Marcus. "Nelson pulls out all the stops. You guys are going to have mad fun down there."

"We're looking forward to it," said Zaria.

Nelson glanced at Jade and asked, "Can I talk to you privately?"

"Sure," replied Jade. Jade and Nelson walked over to the other end of the deck and sat down.

"What's up?" Jade asked.

"I want you and Jordan to come back to Florida with me."

"What? Are you serious?"

"Yes, Jade. I'm falling in love with you," replied Nelson.

"Nelson, I don't know what to say."

"Just say you'll come with me," said Nelson.

"Oh, Nelson. I wish I were as sure as you."

"Jade, that night when I…when we made love was unforgetta-ble. I know you love me, so what are you afraid of?"

"I'm scared that if I fall in love with you, you'll be taken away from me like Connor was."

"Is that what's been holding you back?"

"Pretty much," replied Jade. "I can't go through that pain again, Nelson."

"Jade. No one knows what's gonna happen next week, or next year, but I do know that tomorrow isn't promised to anyone. You deserve to be happy, and I pray that you open your heart to love again because it would be a shame if you didn't."

"I don't know if I can do that, Nelson. I…I'm sorry."

"You don't have to apologize for being honest," said Nelson.

"Are you ready to go back to the fire pit?" Jade asked.

"No. I'm gonna head back to the hotel," replied Nelson.

"Do you really have to leave now?"

"No, but I think it would be best. I'll call you tomorrow."

"Why does this feel so final, Nelson?"

Nelson didn't respond. He stepped closer to Jade, kissed her softly on the cheek, and disappeared into the darkness.

Jade's heart ached as she watched Nelson walk away. She took a few deep breaths and held back the tears that she knew were coming.

One thing she knew for sure was that Nelson loved her and Jordan. He had confessed his love for her over and over. They spent endless nights on the phone, talking into the wee hours of the morn-ing about Connor, psychology, Jordan, and Miami. What was it all for if not for love? If Nelson only knew that with every visit, every feeding, and every phone call, Jade was growing more and more fond of him. Jade wanted Nelson to find love and be loved because he deserved all that love would give him. But Jade didn't tell Nelson any of that. She let him slip away into the darkness and out of her life.

When Jade rejoined her family at the fire pit, they were laugh-ing and carrying on.

"What's so funny?" Jade asked.

"I was telling Zaria about the time you and I were on the bus, and my wig fell off," replied Sophie.

"That was funny as hell." Sophie laughed. "I had to throw that wig back on my head without a mirror. I know I looked rachet."

"Girl, you're a trip," said Jade.

"What's wrong, Jade?" Zaria asked.

"I think Nelson just said goodbye, for good."

"No way. A blind man can see that Nelson is in love with you," said Justin.

"I know. He just told me he was," said Jade.

"And what did you tell him?" Zaria asked.

"That I was scared to fall in love with him."

"Damn, girl," said Justin. "You broke a brother's heart on Christmas."

"Love is love," said Becca. "We can't help who we fall in love with, Jade. Some people never find the kind of love that you and Connor had. You, my friend, found it twice. Never give up on love, Jade."

"Love is love, my ass," said Sophie. "Don't go there, Jade. Connor would turn over in his grave. Brother or no brother, friends don't do that shit to one another."

"Sophie is drunk, Jade, don't mind her," said Becca. "That attitude is exactly why she's single."

"I agree with Becca," said Marcus. "Y'all know I don't say much, but I've spent a lot of time talking to Nelson, and Jade, your brother is right, Nelson loves you."

Jade went inside the house. She saw Mrs. Ellis feeding Jordan and quickly wiped the tears from her face.

"Thanks for feeding her," said Jade.

"No problem at all," said Julia. "Gordon and I are going to be leaving soon, but I want to talk to you before we leave. Sit down, baby.

"I don't know if Nelson ever told you this, but he's like a son to me, and I love him dearly. When Nelson was seventeen, his mother died, and he was devastated. He was the youngest, and he was very close to his mother. When she passed, his father took to the bottle, and his sister didn't help him much because she had a family of her own. No one was there for Nelson, and he needed his family. Nelson was lost and alone, so naturally, I took him under my wing. Nelson spent the whole summer with us, and the bond between him and Connor grew into a brotherhood. And Nelson has been my surrogate son ever since.

"After Connor's funeral, Nelson went to Florida to see his family and then he came to Georgia and stayed with us. He was distraught over Connor's death, because in a way, it was like losing his mother all over again. While Nelson was with us, he told us what happened between him and Connor. Nelson felt bad for not telling anyone about the threats, but he felt worse about lying to Connor. I want you to know that Gordon and I don't blame you or Nelson for what happened. We know you both love Connor very much."

"We do," cried Jade.

"But something else was bothering Nelson. We didn't pry until it got unbearable for us. So the night before Nelson went back to Virginia, we sat him down and had a heart-to-heart with him. We told Nelson that we were not letting him leave until he told us what was bothering him. He laughed at us. Can you believe it? The nerve of that young man."

"What did he tell you?" Jade asked.

"Nelson told us that he was thinking of postponing his internship because he felt like he needed to stay in Virginia and help you and Jordan. We told him that you and Jordan were going to be fine and that he needed to accept the internship.

"Then Nelson told us that he loved you, Jade, and it wasn't easy for him. Nelson didn't want to tell us at all because he felt like he was betraying Connor all over again, but I assured him that he wasn't."

"Mrs. Ellis, I never—"

"Jade, baby, I know. Nelson told us that you were devoted to Connor, and we love you for that."

"He told you that," said Jade.

"Yes," said Julia. "And then Nelson asked us if we had any objections about him being with you."

Julia grabbed Jade's hands and said, "We have no objections. Not one. We gave Nelson our blessing. Love is God's work, Jade, and we dare not mess with his plan."

"But, Mrs. Ellis, I still love Connor."

"Baby, you will always love my son, and he will always love you. Love is knocking at your door once again. Are you going to open it and let love in or shut it and keep love out? The choice is yours. You deserve to be happy, Jade. Connor would want you to be happy. That I know for sure."

"Thank you," said Jade. A tear rolled down Jade's face as she hugged Mrs. Ellis, "Where is Nelson staying?"

"At the Hilton, room 411," shouted her father.

Jade turned around and saw her parents, Justin, and Zaria, standing in the room. Her mother and Zaria were smiling as they held back their tears.

"Thanks, Dad," said Jade.

* * *

When Jade arrived at the Hilton, she felt anxious. She stepped out of the elevator and walked down the hall to Nelson's room. Jade stood outside his door for a few minutes, unsure if she should knock or turn around and go home. She put her ear to the door and heard the faint sounds of the television.

"Good, he's awake," she whispered. Jade knocked on the door.

Nelson opened the door wearing nothing but his black silk pajama pants. He was shocked when he saw Jade. After the shock wore off, he smiled. Nelson reached for Jade's hand and led her inside the room.

The room was dark. The only glimpse of light was the light coming from the television. Nelson took off Jade's coat and threw it on the bed. He faced Jade and admired how the light from the television made her eyes look like crystals.

Nelson stepped closer to Jade. Every vein in his body was on fire. Nelson felt like leaping, but he couldn't move. He stood in the middle of the room admiring Jade's beauty. Neither one of them spoke. Neither one of them knew what came next. The only thing they knew was that they were in love.

Jade looked into Nelson's eyes and whispered the words he longed to hear.

"I'm falling in love with you too, Nelson Parello!"

The end

About the Author

Karon was born and raised in the small town of Bayonne, New Jersey. She attended Henry E. Harris elementary school and later Bayonne High School. While in high school she worked at the local Police Athletic League and volunteered at the Bayonne Youth Center. After graduating Bayonne High School with honors, she was determined to further her education. She enrolled at Jersey City State College, where she majored in Business Management. In 1992, Karon graduated from JCSC, earning her bachelors of science degree in business. She has been fond of writing ever since she was a young girl. Being able to put her thoughts and imagination into words that she can share with others gives her a quiet sense of gratification. As she delivers her second published book, she hopes to share her joy, laughter, and tears of writing with all her readers around the world.

9 781662 448119